Secret of the Samurai Sword

SECRET OF THE SAMURAI SWORD

by Phyllis A. Whitney

PHILADELPHIA

THE WESTMINSTER PRESS

Library of Congress Catalog Card No. 58–8800

PRINTED IN THE UNITED STATES OF AMERICA

For Paul, Jonathan, and David Boorstin, who zestfully introduced me to the life of young Americans in Kyoto.

And with affectionate thanks to Hideo, Toshiko, and Iris Tonomura, who showed me so much of Japan and its people.

Contents

1. The Haunted Garden

HIGH over the Pacific Ocean a plane was winging toward the islands of Japan. Inside its long cabin the stewardess had dimmed the overhead lights so that those passengers who wished to could sleep. In tourist class, up toward the front, she had two special charges — an American boy and girl, who were flying to Japan to spend the summer vacation with their grandmother.

The boy was already asleep, his fair head back against a reclining seat, but the girl only seemed to sleep. The stewardess could not know that her thoughts stirred in excitement and anticipation, keeping her awake. What would Japan be like, Celia was wondering, and this grandmother she could not remember? Tired though she was from the long flight, she kept thinking of picture after attractive picture. They would have a house with a garden, Gran had written. A Japanese house, with a lovely garden . . .

✿

Many miles ahead of the plane, like dark dots upon the ocean, lay the islands of Japan. Above, O-Tsuki Sama, the goddess moon, rode the night sky, bathing the scenes below in soft, shimmering light. On a Kyoto hillside a house waited, still and quiet, as if it held its breath for what was to come. In the garden of the little house something strange moved in the shadows, while across the alley of a narrow street a man in a kimono waited motionless, watching the garden.

He was an old man, with a smooth-shaven head, and even in the pale light there was something noble and benign about his features as he knelt on a cushion beside the rail of a narrow gallery. He watched the garden earnestly, for he knew the other house well and knew that for the moment it stood empty. Yet he was not surprised when he saw movement in the shadows. He had seen this before and knew what to expect. In the warm night, beads of perspiration stood out upon his forehead and his hands gripped the smooth wood of the rail more tightly than he knew.

Beyond the bamboo fence of the house across the way, the shadowy thing stirred and moved softly into the moonlight. Now its garb was evident — that of a samurai, or warrior of feudal days — and the grimacing face shone inhumanly white in the moonlight, the face of one mortally wounded. But so smoothly and silently did it drift across the garden, so swiftly did it vanish from sight, that unless a man were sleepless and watching, the restless spirit of the samurai would never be seen.

The old man was an artist and his senses responded to the shining night, the shimmer of plumy bamboo in the opposite garden, the twisted shadow of a pine tree. His hands slowly relaxed and the sweat dried upon his forehead. The spirit had come and gone, yet he was no wiser than before as to why it came at all, or what it wanted. It had worn no sword and the fact troubled him. A samurai without a sword was like a man without his right arm. Yet despite the puzzle, the old man felt strangely comforted. In the years since the war had ended, there had been much confusion in his soul. But now something from the ancient past was reaching out to touch him. The spirit of Japan still lived — the bombs and the coming of foreigners had not destroyed it.

He went inside his mat room and lay down to sleep, comforted and consoled. More Americans were coming to that house and he could not like the Americans. But at least their presence had not driven away the spirit in the garden.

Nothing moved now in the shadowy space between pine tree and fence. The plumes of bamboo hung quiet in the still air. The house waited in darkness. It could not know that it waited for the coming of a girl. A girl from a distant land, who would hold in her hand the key to all these things.

Over the Pacific flew the plane, its engines roaring steadily, confidently, as the miles sped away.

2. The Flight Bag

IT WAS two days later — a misty noonday, with little sun. The express train from Tokyo to Kyoto sped along the coast line, with the sea on one side and mountains on the other. In the last car Celia and Stephen Bronson occupied a section with their grandmother.

Celia sat next to a window, across from her brother, and watched the paddy fields and tile-roofed villages fly past, hardly able to believe what was happening. Three days ago she and Stephen had been home in Berkeley, California. In the meantime the great Pacific Ocean had been flown and here they were in Japan to visit their grandmother for the summer. A grandmother whom they had not seen since they were practically babies.

Celia glanced at the woman on the seat beside her — the stranger who was her father's mother. And once more she liked the surprise of what she saw. Grandmothers in stories were usually elderly and white-haired. They sat in rocking chairs, knitting. But Monica Bronson's hair was brown and her gray eyes were young and alive. She was as smartly dressed in her blue shantung suit as a model in a fashion magazine, and she wore lipstick and had a touch of color in her cheeks. Celia found it hard to imagine those pretty hands with the rose-tipped nails quietly knitting,

12

but she knew they could fly over the keys of a typewriter. Mrs. Bronson was the author of several travel books about the countries she loved to visit, and this summer she would be writing a book about Japan. Her last book had been an unexpected best seller, and she felt there couldn't be any nicer way to spend extra royalties than to have her grandchildren visit Japan during their vacation. Especially since she would be settled for a time in one place.

Gran caught Celia's glance and smiled at her warmly. " Think you're going to like Japan, Celia? And you, Stephen? "

Stephen answered first, as he usually did. " It will be a good place for taking pictures." He patted the leather case of the camera. He had worked all last summer to get the money to buy it.

Celia smiled at Gran, but let her brother speak for them both. Stephen's hair was as fair as her own shoulder-length fluff, but his eyes were a brighter blue. A lively, sparkling blue. Perhaps " lively " was the best word for Stephen, Celia thought. He always seemed to surge with eagerness and energy — and sometimes impatience. But it was a different sort of eagerness from Celia's. Stephen had an eagerness to be forever moving and doing, while there were times when Celia was happy merely to sit and dream.

Stephen was fifteen, a little more than a year older than his sister. She admired him secretly, and sometimes envied him his assurance and his ability to do so many things well.

"You'll be finding some pictures too, I expect," Gran said to her. " Your mother writes me that you've quite a gift with a pencil and paintbrush. I used to draw a bit when I was young — before I gave it up for writing."

Celia could sense Gran's affection reaching out to her, but she still held back a little, uncertain and not quite sure she could earn that affection. Sometimes a thing you wanted too much seemed to slip away from you like a will-o'-the-wisp. She said nothing about her painting because she thought "gift" was too important a word for her rather unsatisfactory efforts.

Stephen got up suddenly from the red plush seat and began scrabbling through their hand baggage on the rack overhead, as if he'd just thought of something.

"Hey!" he said. "Where's that blue flight bag we brought off the plane yesterday?"

The flight bag! Celia suddenly felt a little sick. She closed her eyes and she could see the bag plainly. She could even see the bag's interior, with Stephen's light meter, his extra supply of film, her own brown loafers, as well as several books she had brought along to read in quiet moments. Yes, she could see it as plainly as though it were there in front of her. Only it wasn't in front of her. It was back in Tokyo right on the closet shelf where she had left it at the hotel. Before she could speak, Stephen gave up his search and looked at her accusingly.

"You were supposed to take care of that bag when Gran went downstairs to pay the hotel bill. I was carrying the heavy things. All you had to do was look after that one little old flight bag. Didn't you bring it from the hotel?"

Celia shook her head mutely. There was no excuse she could offer. It was perfectly true that the responsibility had been hers and that it was a very little thing to look after. But she had been so excited thinking about this trip, and about what Kyoto would be like, that she'd forgotten to take a last look in the closet before she followed Stephen downstairs.

He read the truth in her face and scowled mightily. Gran glanced quickly from one to the other.

"What's the matter, Stephen? Has something been left behind?"

Despairingly Stephen flung himself into his seat. "My light meter's in that bag. Dad gave it to me just last Christmas and it cost plenty. But *she* had to leave it at the hotel. Beautiful but dumb — that's my sister!"

Celia looked out at the flying landscape and blinked her lashes hard. So quickly had he managed to use that hateful phrase in front of Gran. And it *had* been dumb of her to forget the bag.

"It's too bad," Gran said calmly, "but I'll write the hotel a note and we'll mail it when we get to Kyoto. Then the bag can be sent on to us right away."

Stephen continued to glare at Celia. "It'll be fine if somebody steals that meter. The Japs go in for photography and —"

Gran spoke quickly and quietly, but there was something in her tone that Celia had not heard before, and she looked at her grandmother, startled.

"The Japanese are for the most part extremely honest, Stephen. It's quite likely that you'll get the bag back with everything untouched inside it. But in any case, you must remember that when we are the guests of another country, we don't use discourteous terms toward the people of that country."

Stephen wriggled a bit and looked uncomfortable. "O.K.," he said. "I'm sorry." Then he hurried to change the subject. "I'm getting hungry. Do they serve lunch on this train?"

Gran glanced at her watch. "I've a notion about lunch. Of course we can have food in the diner, if you like. But

I think we're coming to a station soon and it might be more fun to get each of us a *bento*. This is a Japanese boxed lunch."

"What sort of lunch is a *bento?*" Stephen asked, but Gran only smiled.

"Wait and see," she said. "Then while we eat I'll tell you something about our house in Kyoto."

Celia turned her attention once more to the flying world outside — the green, wooded mountains, the watery paddy fields, where new green rice was growing. The little square fields were wherever there was a level space, and sometimes they went like steps up a hillside. In their watery surface they mixed the light of the gray sky and turned that greenish too. Always her eye was caught by the little brown figures of men and women, and even children, bent over in a back-breaking position as they worked in the fields.

But now the train was slowing and the outskirts of a town came into view. In a few moments they'd reached the station, and Gran got up quickly and put her hands on the window.

"Here, Stephen, help me open it."

In a moment the window had been flung upward, letting out all the air conditioning of their special car. However, since several others were doing the same thing, it didn't seem to matter. Gran leaned out the opening to call something to a vendor. Celia saw women moving along the platform with trays, piled high with boxes, slung about their necks. Down the length of the train, passengers were leaning out, waving and calling to the vendors.

Gran had been in Japan a number of times and spoke a little Japanese. Now she held up three fingers and spoke a few Japanese words to a vendor. At once three boxes were handed through the window and when Gran had paid for them she beckoned to another woman selling tea. Three small clay teapots were exchanged for a few coins, and Stephen helped bring them inside. On the platform groups of Japanese, some in kimonos, some in Western dress, were hurrying to get aboard, or bowing low to friends who were leaving. Japanese trains, Celia was discovering, did not linger very long in a station and nobody waited if you didn't have your baggage on or off.

Quickly the guard blew a whistle, their train whistled back, and they were off again.

Celia was thankful for the interruption that had taken Stephen's attention and made him forget for the moment the bag left in Tokyo. The box lunches were attractively wrapped in brightly printed paper and tied with paper string. Stephen already had his open and was breaking apart the wooden chopsticks that lay inside. Carefully Celia lifted the thin wooden cover on her box.

The food looked as pretty as a little painted picture. There were neat rolls of rice, speckled with bits of colored vegetable and wrapped in a thin black sheath of what Gran said was seaweed — and really delicious. There were some dabs of brown beans, bits of fish and pickled radish — all as carefully arranged as if the whole thing was to be preserved, instead of eaten right away.

Celia picked up the chopsticks and did her best to imitate Gran in holding them. The beans looked most familiar, so she tried them first. She found them a little like baked beans at home, and quite good. The cold rice and seaweed were surprisingly good too, and so were some of the pickled vegetables. But she couldn't manage the bit of raw pink fish.

" Don't worry," Gran said, wielding her own chopsticks

expertly. "The *bento* was only for fun. Eat what you like and then we'll open the bag of fruit I've brought along. And now I must tell you about the house where we're going to live in Kyoto. It used to belong to a Japanese family that has lived there for many years. But during the Occupation the Army took it over and made some changes. So now it's part Western and part Japanese, and we'll have a real bathroom. The last Americans who occupied it have gone home and I've been able to take it furnished for the summer." She ate a piece of fish and then added cheerfully, "I understand it's supposed to be haunted."

She sounded as though haunted houses were quite common in Japan, and Stephen paused with his chopsticks halfway to his mouth, staring at her in surprise. Gran leaned over to get two of the little clay teapots from the floor beneath her seat, giving one to Celia and the other to Stephen before she picked up her own.

"Do try the green tea and tell me how you like it," she said as calmly as though she had never mentioned a haunted house.

But Stephen was not to be distracted. He dangled the hot bit of pottery by its handle and returned to the point.

"What do you mean — haunted?" he asked in disbelief.

"Oh, people say that queer things happen there." The lid of the teapot was a small cup and she poured hot green liquid into it. "There's supposed to be some sort of apparition that visits the garden. I went down a few weeks ago to have a look at the house and talk to the servants, who are going to stay on with us. The American woman who lived there told me that the Japanese in the neighborhood have some curious notions about the place — though she had never seen or heard anything unusual herself. Maybe we'll be more lucky. I could use a Japanese ghost for my book."

Stephen wrinkled his nose at such nonsense. " I'll have to see a ghost before I'll believe in one," he said.

" So you're a realist, are you? " Gran's gray eyes twinkled. " What about you, Celia? "

Celia hesitated, sipping the green tea and liking its faintly bitter taste. It was sometimes dangerous to speak out her thoughts in front of Stephen — especially when he was mad at her, as he was now. But Gran looked sympathetic.

" I'd rather believe in a ghost than see one," Celia said.

Stephen snorted, but before he could speak, Gran went on: " Don't be so sure that you'll find everything in Japan just the way it is in the States, Stephen. This is a country filled with legends and fantasy. In fact, spirits are so much a part of everyday living in Japan that I'm sure a lot of Japanese don't make very much distinction between what's real and what isn't. Personally, I'm looking forward to a haunted house. Years ago Kyoto was the capital of Japan, and history there goes back into the legendary past."

" Wasn't Kyoto bombed like Tokyo and Yokohama? " Stephen asked.

" Fortunately, no," Gran said. " That's one reason why I'm anxious to stay there and get material for my book. None of the old temples and shrines have been touched, and there is still a lot of ancient Japan to be seen."

Celia wrapped up the lunch box and put it under the seat with the teapot — all of which would be collected at a later station. Then she settled dreamily into her corner beside the window. Except for that matter of the flight bag left in Tokyo, she felt happy and contented. Japan was so beautiful. Even though the sky was misty and the higher, faraway mountains mostly hidden, everything nearby looked like a picture. The small green mountains were as pretty as though they had been carefully arranged for a water color. The graceful pine trees, the lighter green of bamboo thickets, the sudden exclamation point of a red gate leading to a shrine — all added to the charm of the landscape. Already she was longing to capture something of that charm on paper.

Kyoto would be different from busy, noisy Tokyo. She pictured it as a quiet little historic town in the mountains, with all the ladies wearing beautiful kimonos and maybe riding in some of those rickshas which she had read about in books and which had completely vanished from Tokyo.

Most of all, though, she looked forward to the little Japanese house that waited for them. A house with a Japanese ghost haunting it seemed especially picturesque and appropriate. She could imagine a delicate wisp of a Japanese lady ghost. Perhaps a lady who had long ago died for love and continued to return to the garden where she had once been happy. No one could be frightened of such a ghost, or even mind meeting her.

It was a lovely picture.

3. The Girl with the Pony Tail

AT FIRST sight Kyoto was disappointing. It was a sprawling, gray city with busy streets along which people hurried just as they did in Tokyo. Perhaps there was a greater sprinkling of kimonos among them, but most of the women and all the men dressed like Americans.

Gran, Celia, and Stephen carried their bags through the big modern station and found a line of taxis waiting. Not a ricksha in sight. If there were mountains visible, Celia couldn't see them because of the lowering gray sky, mist-laden, which seemed to hover just above the tops of the houses.

First, Gran found a mailbox and dropped in the letter about the flight bag that she'd written on the train. Then they got into a taxi. Gran had a little trouble explaining the address to the driver, because in Japan there were often no house numbers and sometimes not even street names. Fortunately Gran had been here before, so she would know the house without ringing doorbells and asking questions.

The horns, Celia found, were just as noisy as in Tokyo, with every driver blowing like mad practically all the time. At least this didn't look like an American city. There was no mistake about being in Japan. Most of the little

21

shops had open fronts, with all the goods set out in neat rows tilted toward the street so you could see everything at a glance. Everywhere there were attractive, rosy-cheeked children with straight black hair and lively, slanted black eyes. Once, when the taxi stopped at a crossing, children ran to the curb to stare at Celia and Stephen.

"It's because you're so blond," Gran said, and spoke a Japanese greeting to the children. But they only stared at her steadily and didn't answer.

The house was away from the main roads, and the taxi had to slow down as it found its way uphill through streets so narrow they were hardly more than alleys. Their house was the last one on the street, and Gran told the driver where to stop.

"Here we are!" she cried. "Welcome to Kyoto!"

Celia got out of the cab, with Stephen after her, and stood before a tile-roofed wooden gate set in a bamboo fence. Gran rang the bell and paid the driver. In a moment they could hear the clop and scuff of wooden geta as the maid came to open the gate. She was a smiling, round-cheeked little thing in a gray kimono, her black hair bobbed and curled in a neat modern permanent.

"This is Tani-san," Gran said. "Or, as we would say, Miss Tani. She worked for the last Americans who lived here and so did our cook, Setsuko-san. So I know we'll be well taken care of."

Tani smiled and bowed clear to her knees in greeting. Then she reached for the bags Stephen carried, while Setsuko came hurrying out to help with the other baggage. The cook was a gray-haired little woman with snapping black eyes that appraised them at a glance, but did not give away what she thought.

"Men get first attention in Japan," Gran whispered to

Celia as Tani slip-slapped off with Stephen's baggage.

Big, rounded steppingstones led the way through a tiny entrance garden to the front door. The house did not face the street, but stretched its length uphill, parallel with the narrow alley, the bamboo fence running all the way around. It was of unpainted wood like all the Japanese houses, and weathered to a grayish brown. The over-hanging roof was of gray tile, and while the lower floor had conventional Western windows, unlike the sliding doors of other houses on the street, the upper floor was open all the way through.

At the entrance Celia stepped up on a long slab of stone that led to the floor of the entryway. On it were set several pairs of geta and a pair of flat *zori*, or sandals.

" Off with your shoes! " Gran said. She sat down on the entrance floor and removed her shoes.

Stephen got his shoes off first and stepped up onto the polished floor in his socks. When Celia followed she saw an array of bedroom slippers with plastic tops, waiting to be used. She chose a pink pair and then stood looking about the entry hall.

There was nothing to break the clean expanse of darkly shining floor and walls, except a single tall blue vase set in one corner, with purple iris arranged in it. The over-head beam of the entrance was a natural tree branch worked into the ceiling.

" Come along," Gran said. " I'm anxious to show you the house. The mats have all been taken out downstairs and regular floors and walls put in, so we have American furniture down here."

There was a living room and an adjacent dining room that looked like rooms at home. The furniture was low and made of bamboo and rattan, and there were bookcases

set on either side of a Western-style fireplace. Gran led
the way through a modern kitchen with a small brown
wooden icebox in it.

On the other side of the entryway, connecting with it
through the kitchen, steep narrow stairs ran upward to
the second floor. The stairs were uncarpeted and slippery,
so Celia clung to the long bamboo rail that ran up the wall.

Tani had left her geta on the stone step outside and
wore something on her feet that looked like white cloth
mittens, the big toe separated from the rest. Inside she
walked around in these *tabi*.

Upstairs there were three rooms set in a row, with a
narrow, open veranda running around them, serving as a
hallway. The rooms themselves had the traditional straw
matting laid over the floors. *Tatami*, Gran said the mats
were called. Light wheat-colored matting was fastened
together in squares by strips of black binding cloth. Celia
found the matting springy beneath her feet and not at all
hard. The three rooms were separated by fusuma, thin
walls that slid in grooves, as did the doors, and they were
almost bare of furniture.

"Where do we keep our clothes and things?" Stephen
asked, looking about curiously. "Where do we sleep?"

Tani understood a little English and she padded to a
sliding door and moved it on its track, revealing a closet.

"Usually," Gran explained, "Japanese fold everything
away on shelves, but a few shelves have been removed
from these cupboards so we can hang up our clothes. You
can see the bedding piled there on the remaining shelves.
Suppose I take this end room and you the one in the middle, Celia. Then Stephen can have the one beyond."

It seemed a good plan, and they went into their own
rooms to unpack. Slippers were left outside on the veranda

floor and one walked on the *tatami* only in socks or stockings. With no chairs and no waist-high tables, it was necessary to sit on the floor for whatever you wanted to do, including the unpacking of a suitcase.

Celia found there were just two pieces of furniture in her room. One was a low oval table of reddish lacquer set in the middle of the room. The other was a curious little dressing table. A green silk cushion lay on the matting before it and Celia went down on her knees to examine the dresser more closely.

It sat right on the floor, without legs, and was almost like a doll's dressing table. A narrow mirror, perhaps two feet high, with a cloth cover over it, rose above a small ledge, and there were three small drawers in a tier at one side. The surface was a reddish-brown lacquer with traces of gold decoration. But the lacquer was old and there were cracks and chips in it here and there.

"I thought you'd like that," Gran said, looking in from the veranda. "I found it downstairs in a room that's been used for storage. I suppose it was discarded because the lacquer's chipped, but I think it's rather nice." She nodded at Celia and went back into her own room.

Celia pulled out the little drawers of the dresser by the brass rings of their handles. The top two were empty, but there was something in the bottom drawer. She reached in and took out an oblong box of black lacquer.

It was a small box, with a beautiful little pine tree painted in gold on its surface, its long needles done in feathery gold strokes. Little clusters of gold needles lay on the ground beneath the tree. It would be a lovely box to keep bits of jewelry in and she took the top off to look inside. The box was empty, but it too looked old and a little battered, and there were some scratches on the shallow bottom. Celia put her find back in the drawer and crossed the room to the narrow rear veranda.

She could unpack any time, but now she wanted to see what might be glimpsed of Kyoto. This part of the house looked out upon garden and green hillside, with other smaller houses visible to the right across the narrow street. What had been only a hint of garden at the front of their house ran along one side and opened into something that had the delicacy of a Japanese print.

Below the veranda rail was a small fish pond, with the glint of goldfish darting beneath the surface of the water. Again there were steppingstones and a small, symmetrical stone lantern. A pine tree as graceful as the one on the lacquer box grew beside the lantern, and in one corner of the garden was a feathery clump of bamboo. There were no flower beds, but a flowering bush of red azalea gave the garden a note of bright color. The scene was one that made Celia long to paint it. She could imagine what the garden would look like on a moonlit night. It would be a perfect place for the gentle kimono-clad ghost of her imagination.

Only one ugly note spoiled the perfection. In the middle of the garden, beyond the fish pond, rose an ugly lump of rounded concrete. It stood several feet high and looked completely out of place.

Before she turned away, she looked across to the two-storied Japanese houses that lined the street. They too were weathered to a grayish brown, with sloping gray roofs. In some of them reed blinds hung in the upper rooms to shut out the afternoon glare.

As she watched, a blind in the last house across the street was pushed aside and a Japanese girl stepped out on the veranda. She bent to examine several plants set on a

wooden ledge, but Celia suspected that she only pretended her interest in them, because every now and then
she cast a sidelong glance in Celia's direction.

The girl wore a green blouse and a brown cotton skirt,
and while there were the same black bangs across her
forehead that many Japanese girls wore, her long hair was
drawn back to form a pony tail behind. In Tokyo, Celia
had seen a number of girls on the street wearing their hair
in that fashion, so it wasn't too unusual. But this girl
flipped it about as she moved her head in a gesture that
seemed almost American.

If she knew the word in Japanese, Celia thought, she
might call hello to the other girl. In fact, why shouldn't
she just call hello anyway, even if she didn't know how to
say it in Japanese?

She waved her arm to get the other girl's attention and
received a surprised look in return.

" Hi! " Celia called. " Hello! "

For just a moment she thought the Japanese girl might
smile in return. But then an elderly man in a gray kimono
stepped out on the veranda beside her. His head was as
completely bald as if it had been shaved, and he looked
rather distinguished and dignified. He spoke quietly to
the girl, who turned and went inside as if in obedience to
his words.

Gran must have heard Celia's call, for she came out to
see what was happening. At sight of the old man on the
opposite veranda, she made a polite bow. But though he
returned the bow gravely, he did not smile and he went
inside at once. The reed blind swung behind him and the
other house was still.

Celia was puzzled. " He didn't seem very friendly. I
don't think he wanted that girl to talk to me."

"We're strangers and he doesn't know us yet," Gran said. "He looks like an important person to me, because of his bearing and that fine kimono he was wearing. Most men these days wear Western dress in Japan, or else in summertime they get into cotton *yukata* at home. The *yukata* is the comfortable summer kimono everyone wears. Well, we'll go slowly and not push. You'll find most Japanese ready to be friendly."

Celia felt disappointed. There weren't likely to be many American girls in Kyoto, and the girl with the pony tail had looked as though she would be fun to know.

Tani came upstairs with word that a visitor was at the door to see them. From a house in the neighborhood, she indicated.

Gran laughed. "It's started sooner than usual. I've a few more things I want to do. Celia, can you leave your unpacking and go downstairs?"

Celia could leave her unpacking easily enough, but she was hesitant about going down to meet a stranger.

Gran patted her shoulder. "Run along. You'll probably make a new friend. And I'll send Stephen down to join you."

Thus urged, Celia went downstairs and into the living room. A Japanese boy of about seventeen stood in the middle of the room, examining with interest some books Gran had dropped on the table when she came in. He wore the dark trousers and white shirt of the student, and there were round-lensed glasses with horn rims hooked over his ears. When he saw Celia he snapped to attention and made her a courteous bow.

"Good morning, sir," he greeted her, though the sun was already slipping down the sky. "Prease to excuse me if I am coming so fast."

Celia blinked and said, "Hello," uncertainly.

The young man bowed again. " Name is Hiro Sato. I am coming here to rearn Engris." And now he beamed at her, smiling broadly.

It was a good thing Stephen appeared in the doorway just then. At the sight of another boy, Hiro looked delighted. He bowed again and repeated the words with which he had greeted Celia.

Stephen rose to the occasion. " Sure, I'll teach you English," he said, grinning in amusement. " First of all, you don't say, ' Good morning ' when it's practically evening. You say, ' Good evening.' Or you can just say, ' Hello.' "

Hiro drew in his breath. " ' Harro,' I know how to say," he told them with dignity.

" That's not right," said Stephen. " Why don't you sit down and we'll try that again."

They were still trying the " *l* " sound that was so difficult, since the Japanese have no such sound in their language, when Gran joined them. She said, " *Komban wa*," which Celia thought meant " good evening," and exchanged a few words with the boy in his own language.

" Hiro is anxious to practice his English and learn more of the language," she explained. " He lives near here, and I gather that he wanted to get to us before anyone else did. Students learn a little English in school, but they don't have much chance to use it. Perhaps if you help him, he'll teach you some Japanese."

" Ask him if he plays baseball," Stephen requested.

But Hiro knew that word. " *Beso-boru!* " he said, and jumped up to make a catching motion in the air. Then he realized what he had done, blushed, and sat down again looking self-conscious.

Tani, who had been watching, murmured to Gran, " Soon comes dinner."

Hiro must have understood the word because he stood

up at once, profusely apologetic, and started for the door.

"Come over tomorrow," Stephen invited, and Hiro bowed again delightedly, put on his shoes and hurried out the gate.

Stephen laughed out loud. "Wow! What an oddball. Do you suppose he really knows anything about baseball?"

Gran looked as if she might say something rather sharp to Stephen and then changed her mind. "The Japanese are great baseball fans," she said mildly. "And it may be that he can teach you a few things."

Tani announced dinner and they went to the table. Setsuko knew American tastes, and the meal was good. Afterward Celia went upstairs and unpacked. Most of her things fitted into the closet and on the shelves, but she left her painting and sketching kit out because she would probably want to use these things in the morning. As she worked, Tani came in with a bow and began laying out the thick padded quilts that would make her bed for the night. Accompanying the maid was a rangy, ginger-colored cat which was plainly at home in the house. Celia, who loved cats, went down on her knees and held out her hand to make its acquaintance. The cat sniffed her fingers impersonally and went off about the room on a tour of inspection.

"Cat belong Setsuko-san," Tani said. "All time hungry."

"What's its name?" Celia asked.

Tani was on her knees spreading out one layer after another of thick quiltlike padding. She bent double, laughing as though Celia had said something funny.

Gran called out an explanation. "I understand that wherever Setsuko-san takes the cat, the American family she works for gives it a new name. So she just calls it

'Neko-chan,' which is 'little cat' in Japanese."

The ginger cat evidently didn't understand her pronunciation of its name, for it yawned and sat down to wash its face.

It was growing darker outside, and Celia gave up trying to make friends with the cat. She went to the veranda rail to look into the garden again. No moon lighted the misty sky, but she could still make out the graceful shape of the pine tree and the glimmering mirror of the fish pond. Then she saw something stooped and strange that startled her for just a moment. It had seemed as though something ghostly was huddled down there in the dark garden. She looked again more closely and saw that it was only the hulk of concrete she had noticed earlier.

At her soft exclamation, Tani left her bedmaking and came to her side.

"*Nan desu ka?*" the maid asked. "What is matter?"

"What's that concrete thing down in the garden?" Celia asked the maid.

Tani peered into the dusk. "For *bakudan*," she said. Then, noting Celia's puzzlement, she stretched out her arms like the wings of a plane and sailed up and down the veranda making a buzzing noise. "Boom, boom, boom!" she finished triumphantly.

Celia understood. The people of Kyoto hadn't known they wouldn't be bombed and had probably built shelters, like everyone else in Japan. Now the ugly thing remained to spoil the lovely garden. Thinking of the garden reminded her of another question.

"Is the garden really haunted, Tani-san?" she asked.

The little maid smiled at her happily, but without comprehension.

"You know — ghosts," Celia went on. "Spirits." The difficulty of getting through the barrier of language was making itself felt again. She couldn't think of any way to describe a ghost with gestures, as Tani had done with an airplane.

She went down the veranda to her grandmother's room and looked in. Gran had changed to a comfortable blue-and-white cotton *yukata* and was sitting on a cushion before the low lacquer table in her room, spreading some papers out upon it. When she saw Celia her eyes crinkled up in smile lines.

" What is the Japanese word for ghost? " Celia asked.

Gran didn't know, but she had a small red dictionary at hand and she looked up the word. " Here it is — *o-b-a-k-e*. Pronounced ' oh-bah-kay.' Let me know if you find out anything about our private ghost. It has to go into my book."

Celia went back to Tani. " What I mean is — do you think an *o-bake* really comes to the garden? "

"*O-bake* — in garden? " Tani repeated nervously. " Maybe so." Then she looked at the cat. "Onry Neko-chan see *o-bake*."

The ginger cat paid no attention to this talk about ghosts. If it had any interest in whatever haunted the garden, it did not reveal it. But when it got up to follow Tani as she went to make the bed in Stephen's room, Celia looked after it with amused respect. A cat that saw ghosts might be worth cultivating.

4. Encounter Near the Shrine

THAT NIGHT Celia snuggled between her layers of Japanese *futon* and found sleeping on the floor a comfortable and cozy experience. The *tatami* was so springy to begin with that it wasn't like sleeping on a hard floor. She wished Mom and Dad could see her strange bed.

Stephen must have felt the same way, because he called out to her softly through the thin fusuma that separated their rooms, "Hey, Celia — you asleep?"

"No, I'm not," she whispered back.

"Wouldn't Mom and Dad flip over this place? Wish they were here."

"So do I," Celia said, and felt comfortingly close to Stephen.

It was nice to have an older brother, even if he didn't always approve of her. When they were little she'd tagged around after him and thought he was smarter than any other boy, and better at doing everything. He'd played with her more then, and sometimes he used to stick up for her with the other kids. But of course they'd grown up since then, and Mom said things couldn't very well stay the same between them. Though perhaps here in Japan, when they were such a long way from home . . . If only she hadn't forgotten that flight bag!

33

She spoke to him again softly. " Are you still mad about the bag? Honestly, I'm sorry — "

" O.K., O.K.," he broke in. " But it was such a little thing to remember."

So he was still upset about it, and she couldn't blame him. It was true that she sometimes did the dumbest things. Mostly because she was thinking about something else, or too excited to think at all. Stephen never understood about that.

Well, she would just have to do better here. And perhaps she really could if she tried hard enough. She fell asleep still sorry about the bag and a little homesick too. With the whole Pacific Ocean between, her parents and home seemed very far away.

Once during the night Celia wakened and listened to the night sounds of Kyoto. In the distance the horns of trucks and taxis continued their insistent uproar. It was a good thing this house was up a side street here on the hill where little traffic came through.

From a balcony near at hand drifted plaintive strains of music played on some unfamiliar stringed instrument. Over and over again, plink, plink-plink, striking the same few sad, strange notes, sounding utterly lonely in the quiet street. Now and then a clopping sound went past the house, and at first Celia couldn't figure it out. Then she remembered the geta — the wooden clogs she had seen on so many Japanese feet — and knew they would make just such a sound. Still closer, in the garden, insects chirped and buzzed endlessly. She had not known the night could be filled with so many sounds. At home in Berkeley she didn't notice night noises at all. Being used to them, she didn't even hear boat whistles or foghorns out in the bay.

If it hadn't been so comfortable and cozy beneath her

quilts, she might have crept out of bed and gone barefoot across the *tatami* to the veranda to look down upon the garden. Perhaps if she were lucky one of these nights, she might catch the gentle little Japanese ghost who sometimes came there. She smiled to herself at the whimsy, and her eyelids drooped sleepily. Somewhere on a nearby street sounded the mournful notes of a street vendor's flute. The little tune was haunting, and she wanted to remember it. But she fell asleep before the few notes were within her grasp.

She slept longer than she meant to in the morning and was wakened by something sniffing in her ear. She opened her eyes to look into the yellow gaze of the ginger cat. It mewed in friendly fashion and ran a sandpaper tongue over her hand. At the same moment, Gran came along the veranda ready for the day.

"*O-hayo gozaimasu,* Celia-san," she said. "That means a very polite good morning to you. Your brother is already up and around, and Setsuko-san is ready to start the bacon and eggs."

"I'll get up right away," Celia said, and scrambled out from under the covers. She dressed quickly and then went out to the front veranda to have a look at Kyoto in the daytime. Thin sunshine had broken through the clouds, and now she could see for a considerable distance. The city occupied a great plain and all around it were wooded mountains. Their own hillside was at the foot of a steep, tree-covered slope.

Kyoto was still a city of gray roof tops, but now she could see green sections of trees, and here and there the red flash of a shrine or temple. In one place, standing up in plain view and towering above everything near it, was an enormous red gate which Gran said meant the approach to a Shinto shrine. The Japanese, it seemed, had two kinds of religion, somewhat mixed up together — Buddhism and Shinto. The Buddhists had temples, the Shinto sects shrines, but often a Japanese would belong to both groups at once.

Now she could smell bacon frying, and discovered that she was ravenously hungry. So she hurried down the stairs, her pink plastic slippers flapping against the polished wood. At the breakfast table Gran talked about plans for the day. She had put on harlequin glasses with blue rims to examine an opened-out map.

"I'm sorry I can't be with you much this morning — I've had to arrange several appointments with people who are hard to catch. But you'll both find plenty to do. I've marked the location of our house on this map so you can tell where you are. I know you'll want to explore, but for a few days don't wander too far from home. After I've had a chance to take you downtown and you have a better idea of the city, then you can go where you like. You're perfectly safe anywhere. The Japanese love children and they're always especially kind to foreign visitors. If you get lost, you can hop in a taxi and show the driver the map. The small, sixty-yen taxis are almost as cheap as buses or streetcars at home."

After breakfast Celia went to the front gate of the house and stood in its tile-roofed opening, watching the children go off to school. The Japanese school term was long, with little time allowed for vacation, so classes were still in session.

Although their street ended at the top of the hill, another narrow street crossed it at the top and ran parallel to the hill behind the house. From this street came boys and girls of all ages, joining others who poured in from their street. The girls wore dark skirts and white blouses, the boys dark trousers and white shirts. A good many of the girls had their hair cut in a straight bob, with black bangs across the forehead. The older boys wore black caps with visors. Most of the children had on shoes and socks, but there were still many with bare feet in geta.

As they hurried past Celia, the girls whispered and threw shy glances her way. The boys nudged each other and laughed. She stood in the gateway watching until, far down the hill, the road was a sea of black and white figures.

The sight made her feel a little lonely. Here were hundreds of boys and girls she couldn't talk to. How could you ever make friends when you couldn't make the simplest words understood? She glanced across the street toward the house she had noted the night before, and saw that the girl she had seen on the upstairs veranda stood in her own gateway. She was not dressed in the uniform the schoolgirls wore, but had on a green cotton summer dress. She too was watching the sea of boys and girls pour out of adjacent streets and join the stream in the wider main street below. Celia wondered why she wasn't going to school along with the others. Once the girl glanced in her direction, but then looked quickly away. After the behavior of the old man last night, Celia did not attempt to smile at her again.

As the other girl waited, two little girls and a boy ran out of the house. They did not wear the uniforms of the bigger school children, but ordinary Western dress. The two little girls tugged at the older girl's skirt, to pull her into the street, but she held back, waiting. A few more children from the alley above went past and Celia saw that they stared at the Japanese girl almost as strangely as they stared at her, and that she did not speak to any of them. Perhaps she was a newcomer here too, Celia thought. In which case they certainly ought to be friends.

It was the little boy, who must have been about six, who settled matters. He gave his two sisters, who were smaller than he, a good rough push from behind and chattered something commanding in Japanese to the older girl. She shook her head at him, and he would have pushed her too, but she reached out suddenly and caught his hand. Then she lifted him up in the air and gave him a good shaking before she set him on his feet again. He opened his mouth in astonishment and anger and screamed lustily, while his two little sisters shrank back against the gate and stared at the older girl in dismay. The boy's screams brought a woman running out of the house to catch him up and soothe his tears.

Although she couldn't understand a word that was said, Celia could see exactly what the pantomime meant. The boy was wailing to his mother about Big Girl's rude treatment. His mother appeared to be murmuring indignant words to the girl and directing her down the street, though she didn't raise her voice at all, and her manner remained polite. Celia was inclined to side with the girl for shaking the rough little boy.

The older girl said nothing, but she didn't look a bit contrite. She held out her hands to the two little girls and started down the hill, with the boy running on ahead, laughing now and taunting her. Not once did she glance Celia's way, though she probably knew that the whole affair had been witnessed by the American girl across the street.

There was something strange going on in that house, Celia thought as she left the gate and went around to the rear garden.

Stephen had just come out of the house with his camera slung about his neck, and Gran behind him. For the first time Stephen spied the concrete hulk in the middle of the garden and went over to give it a slap.

"What's this stuck up here for?" he asked.

"I think it's a bomb shelter," Gran said. "It doesn't help the looks of the garden, does it? Most Japanese simply dug caves in the hard clay earth, and those have been filled in since the war. But a thing like this is harder to get rid of."

"Wonder what's down there?" Stephen said. He walked around the lump of concrete, and Celia, following him, saw that there was a door set into the other side. Stephen turned the knob and shook it, but it was plainly locked and he gave up without further interest.

"Are you off for some picture-taking?" Gran asked.

Stephen nodded. "Might as well get started, though it will be tough in this light with no meter."

"Don't you want to go along, Celia?" Gran asked.

She did, of course, but Stephen was thinking about that flight bag again, and he might not want her. She looked at him a little anxiously.

"O.K., come along," he said, not sounding enthusiastic, but not turning her down either.

Gran seemed not to notice his tone. She nodded briskly. "That's fine. I think it might be a good idea, Celia, for you to stay with Stephen your first few trips away from the house."

"I'll go get my sketching things," Celia said quickly, and flew toward the house before Stephen could change his mind.

Dashing in and out of a house in Japan wasn't as simple as at home. There was always the matter of taking off one's shoes — which she nearly forgot. But Tani was there to catch her and see that she put on slippers. By the time she and Stephen started down the hill, the girl from across the street was out of sight with her charges.

Just after they left the house, a strange-looking three-wheeled truck came up the hill. The front part was built like a motorcycle, even to the handles the driver held, though he sat inside a closed cab. The back was a tiny truck. The whole thing came toward them with the loud noises of a motorcycle, and Stephen grinned as they flattened themselves against a bamboo fence to let it by.

" That's a *bata-bata*," he said. " The Japanese call them *bata-bata* because that's the sort of noise they make."

This one was delivering tiny, six-ounce milk bottles to their house, since that was the only size in which pasteurized milk could be purchased.

Their street opened onto a wider one now, but there were still no sidewalks. The road followed the contour of the hill, running at length into a pleasant park, with benches set around invitingly, and a decorative bridge arched over a pond of water.

Stephen stopped to take a picture, and Celia strolled downhill toward what looked like the buildings of a shrine. Traffic turned off at this point, but pedestrians were using the area as a thoroughfare, so there was clearly nothing private about it. There were buildings here and there with tiled roofs that curved up into sharp horns at the corners, and on the far side down the slope of the hill was a great red structure with a tiled roof that made an imposing entrance to the area.

Celia wandered along, fascinated, wondering what she would most like to draw. A paved courtyard opened up around a turn and she stopped in amazement. Thirty or forty children had spread out all over the courtyard and were sitting happily on the stones with large sheets of drawing paper spread out before them. Every child was busily painting one or another of the views to be seen in the parklike shrine about them. The paintings were really very good for children of their age, Celia saw, and she was interested in the tubes of water colors they were using.

The teacher noticed Celia and smiled at her.

" Hello," Celia said, longing to speak to someone, and at the sound of her voice a number of the children looked up from their work and stared at her with unblinking black eyes. The teacher spoke to them, and the girls wrenched their fascinated gaze away and concentrated on their work again. The boys were less docile than the girls. They grinned at her saucily, and some of them tried out the word " harro " among themselves.

Celia wished she could look more closely at the paintings, but she didn't want to disrupt the class any further.

Stephen came toward her down the hill, and she waved him away from the outdoor art class for fear he would go tramping through it. A walk shaded by pine trees paralleled the courtyard, and Celia moved toward it. She had seen a bench there in the shade, half concealed by shrubbery, and she knew now just what she wanted to draw.

" Why don't you get some more pictures? " she said to her brother. " I'll stay here and wait for you and do some sketching."

Stephen was all for an arrangement that would leave him unhampered, and he went off without making his usual remarks about how long it took to get one picture when you had to draw it.

Celia seated herself on the stone bench and opened her sketchbook. If she could just capture on paper a semblance of those kneeling, squatting figures, so absorbed in their painting, with the curved roof of a shrine building in the backgound, it would make an interesting picture.

Her pencil moved on the paper. In this corner she could put in a branch of a pine tree, just as it hung over her head. And beyond the kneeling children she would draw a little stone lantern like the one in the garden of their Kyoto house. That was the thing Stephen never understood about painting a picture. You could use your imagination and add what wasn't there, or change what was, so that you ended up with something you had created yourself. That seemed much more satisfying than just pointing a camera and snapping the shutter. Though of course Stephen had his own notions about that.

In no time she was as absorbed as the children she was drawing, and she didn't notice the encroaching wave of watchers until it had practically surrounded her. When one of the toddlers came around in front and stared right into her face, his mouth slightly open in amazement over this strange phenomenon of a human being with yellow hair and blue eyes and such queer features, Celia looked up and saw that she was again the center of attention.

A collection of small children had gathered around her to stare, and beyond them were even some grownups, their attention caught by an American girl drawing, but not by the children beyond her in the courtyard. The watchers made a friendly, smiling group, but they kept edging a little closer until Celia knew she would have to stop, because she couldn't draw with a crowd around her. And she didn't know how to tell them to go away, and felt that would be impolite anyway. So she closed the sketchbook, hoping that would make them lose interest, but it didn't in the least. They were quite happy to continue staring, as if they had never seen anything so remarkable before and were never likely to again.

There was, she decided, nothing to do but give up her project and walk away. But before she could move, a girl came through the circle of watchers, clapping her hands right and left at the children and speaking rapidly in Japanese. Her black pony tail swung and joggled with the energy of her movements and Celia saw in surprise that it was the girl from the house across the alley.

Reluctantly the throng of small children gave up staring and returned to their play, and the grownups smiled and went off in whatever direction they were headed. When she had dispersed the whole group, the other girl made a dusting gesture of brushing her palms together. Then she put her hands on her hips and stared at Celia herself, unsmiling and plainly as interested as any of the little ones had been.

Somehow, Celia knew, she had to thank this girl for rescuing her. Haltingly she struggled with the phrase she had heard Gran use to Tani that morning, and which she had practiced later.

" A-arigato go-gozaimashita," she stammered, and hoped that her pronunciation wasn't too awful for the other girl to understand.

For the first time the Japanese girl smiled in amusement. " Oh, that's O.K.," she said. " You're perfectly welcome."

Her accent was as American as Celia's own, and it was startling to hear there in the courtyard of a Kyoto shrine.

5. The Dying Samurai

FOR A MOMENT Celia stared at the other girl in astonishment. "But — but you *are* Japanese?" she managed at length.

The girl tossed her head, and the pony tail bounced rebelliously. "I'm not Japanese — I'm American! I'm just as Amercian as you are. I was born in San Francisco and I've lived there all my life. Until a month ago. Now I'm here." She flung out her hands, taking in all of Kyoto with a scornful gesture.

"But — you speak Japanese," Celia faltered.

"Sure, I speak it. I can't help it that my parents were Japanese and taught it to me when I was little. But I'm American, and I'm not going to let anyone forget it."

"It's wonderful to hear somebody speak English," Celia murmured, wanting to lessen the other girl's indignation. "I wondered why you didn't go to school with the others this morning."

"I don't want to go to school here," the girl said, and changed the subject quickly. "Where do you live in the States? And what's your name? Mine is Sumiko Sato."

"Mine's Celia Bronson," Celia told her. "And I've always lived in Berkeley, right across the bay from San Francisco — so we're neighbors."

"In more ways than one." Sumiko sat down on the

bench beside Celia. " But I'll have to be careful about talking to you back there," she added, nodding toward the direction in which they both lived. " My grandfather doesn't like Americans."

" I saw what happened yesterday," Celia confessed. " He told you to go into the house when I waved, didn't he? Is it because of the war that he doesn't like us? "

Sumiko shrugged. " He's very old-fashioned. I don't understand half of what he's talking about. All that stuff he goes for about ancestors and old Japan. But just because Hiro's a boy, he didn't say a word when he went over to see if you would teach him English."

" Hiro? You mean the Japanese boy who came to see us yesterday? "

" Yes. Hiro Sato is my cousin. Our fathers were brothers."

This was growing confusing. " I should think Hiro would get you to teach him English, since you speak it so well."

Sumiko's black eyes snapped. She too seemed anxious to talk to someone in her native tongue. " He thinks he's special because he's a boy. I should think by now Japan would be over the idea that boys are better than girls. But of course Gentaro Sato would encourage him in that notion."

" Gentaro Sato? "

" My grandfather. Everyone says he is a very distinguished man in Japan. Quite a famous artist. But he's old-fashioned about his art too. He only draws nature in the classic manner. They say that all through the war he sat in his room painting bees and blossoms. What a bore! But I liked what you were doing just now — may I see? "

" I've only just started," Celia said, but she opened her sketchbook and showed the page to Sumiko. She had blocked in the general scene, and in one place she had started drawing a little girl, squatting on her haunches as she used a paintbrush on her paper.

"I should think everyone would want to draw people," Sumiko said. "But if you look at those things the kids are painting out there, you'll see they're mostly temples and trees, with hardly ever a human being in them. Sometimes I think the Japanese don't really want anyone to be a *person*. My grandfather thinks everyone *must* fit a pattern that's been followed for hundreds of years."

She jumped up restlessly, completely American in her manner, in her every gesture. Yet Celia could not entirely accept her words. It seemed as if Sumiko was decidedly prejudiced against the Japanese.

"I've only been in Japan a few days," Celia said quietly. "But so far I love it. My grandmother has been here several times and she always comes back because she likes it so much. She's even writing a book about Japan."

"That's all right for her. And for you too." Sumiko reached toward a pine branch over her head and broke off a sprig of needles and held it to her nose. "You can all go home whenever you like. But not me. I've got to stay here for ages — maybe all my life. My grandfather wants to turn me into a proper Japanese girl, but I'm a nisei and I'll never fit in out here. I don't want to!"

As Celia knew, a nisei was a person who was born in America of Japanese parents. Sumiko sounded so upset that Celia felt sorry for her.

"What about your parents?" she asked. "Don't they want to go back to America?"

"Not my mother. She grew up here in Kyoto and she has always wanted to come home. So when my father died —" Sumiko blinked hard for a moment, "that was just six months ago — she sold his greenhouse and prepared to come back to Japan. I wanted to stay behind, but I'm only fourteen and they wouldn't let me. If I were older, I might have found a job. I wanted to go to the university in Berkeley." She tossed the sprig of pine away. " I suppose I'd better get back to the house or they'll be wondering what happened to me. I went out to take my little cousins to the nursery school."

" Do you mind if I walk back with you? " Celia said.

Sumiko seemed pleased, so Celia looked about for Stephen and saw him taking a picture of an old woman in front of a priest who was telling fortunes. As they walked toward him, the priest handed the woman a slip of white paper which she read anxiously. Then she shook her head in displeasure and went over to a nearby bush, where she tied the strip of paper to a twig. Celia saw that hundreds of other strips had been tied to the same bush at one time or another.

" Why is she doing that? " she asked Sumiko.

" It was a bad fortune, so she's throwing it away by fastening it to that bush. Such superstition! "

" Gran says that people do seem to mix up the real and the unreal a lot in this country," Celia said. " Even at our place there's supposed to be a spirit that sometimes appears in the garden at night."

Sumiko threw her a quick look, but for once she didn't seem so sure of herself, or so ready to comment. Indeed, she appeared a little uneasy. But before Celia could ask if she had heard something too, Stephen saw them and came over. Celia enjoyed his surprised look when she introduced Sumiko and the girl spoke to him in English.

Since Stephen didn't want to leave as yet, Celia and Sumiko started up the hill together. They went slowly and looked at things along the way. There was a row of stalls in the shrine grounds, selling inexpensive articles for passers-by, and the two girls stopped to look at the neat array of post cards, balls, whistles, pencils, candy, and other assorted articles. There was even a small flower stand, and Celia stopped before it in delight.

"Look at all the little bunches of flowers!" she said. "There aren't any flowers in our garden, so I think I'll buy a bunch for my grandmother. If they're not too expensive."

"They are sweet," Sumiko said. "Maybe I'll take my mother a bunch too."

She asked the price, and the girls found they had enough coins in their pockets to make the modest purchase. They walked on, each carrying a little bunch of flowers and sniffing at it now and then.

Celia was still thinking about the uneasiness with which Sumiko had greeted her remark about the spirit in the garden, and now she returned to this subject.

"Have you heard about it too?" she asked directly. "I mean about the ghost in our garden?"

Sumiko hesitated for just a moment. "My grandfather says he's seen it. He thinks —" she shook her head and broke off. "I'm not going to believe in ghosts until I see one."

"You're like Stephen," Celia said, and let the topic go. She was beginning to feel that she knew the little ghost rather well, and she didn't want anyone to say harsh things about her.

As they walked uphill, Sumiko returned to her own problem. "America was where my father wanted me to grow up. I — I miss him such a lot." Her voice broke again, and then she went on quickly to hide her emotion. "My mother came out from Japan as a girl to marry my father, and she is different. I suppose it was difficult for my grandfather to lose his younger son to another country. And then his elder son, Hiro's father, died right after the war."

"Were those your grandfather's only two children?" Celia asked.

"He has one daughter left — my little cousins' mother. Their father is working down in the south of Japan and isn't home with us just now. Anyway, with both his sons gone, my grandfather is all the more determined that his grandchildren must grow up as proper Japanese. But I'm not going to be pushed into the pattern he wants to set for me."

As far as Celia could see, there wasn't any way out of her new friend's predicament.

The road curved pleasantly along the hillside, and every few moments a *bata-bata* or motorcycle or automobile went roaring past with a great tooting of its horn. Celia felt nervous about the lack of sidewalks and walked along the very edge of the road.

When they reached the narrow beginning of their alley, they paused before the open front of a small store. There were trays of candy, fruit, Japanese cakes, bread, odds and ends of groceries, pencils and notebooks, and household supplies. A woman with a white apron over her kimono and her kimono sleeves tied back with cords over her shoulders smiled at Sumiko and stared with interest at Celia. She spoke to Sumiko in Japanese, and the two had quite a discussion. When the girls walked on, Sumiko smiled.

"She wanted to know if you dye your hair to get it that color, the way the stars in the *shinema* — the movies — do. She didn't think it could really grow that way. Here in

Kyoto they don't see as many foreigners as they do in Tokyo — so you'll be stared at more."

" I know," Celia said, and they laughed together.

But as they neared their own neighborhood, Sumiko sobered. "Maybe I'd better go ahead alone. If I come right up to the house with you, Grandfather will be upset again." She looked at Celia wistfully. " Do you think we — I mean, would you want to — "

" Oh, do let's see each other again," Celia said quickly.

She had a feeling that Sumiko felt a little lost between her two worlds. Probably the Japanese didn't quite accept or approve of her because she seemed American to them. Yet she looked Japanese and would never be taken for an American by foreigners.

" I'll watch for the times when you're out with the children," Celia promised. " I didn't know I'd be so lucky as to meet someone here who speaks English. We'll have fun together this summer."

Sumiko's whole face brightened. " That will be wonderful. Be seeing you." She ran ahead up the hill and left Celia to follow more slowly.

" *Sayonara*," said Celia softly after her. She knew the good-by word, at least.

On ahead, she saw Sumiko reach the gate of her house and saw Hiro come out of it at just that moment. Sumiko held up the flowers to show her cousin, and he burst out laughing right in her face. He was still laughing as he came down the hill toward Celia. Sumiko stared at the little bouquet for a moment, and then with a sudden angry gesture tossed it in the gutter that ran beside the alley. Without a backward look she went into the house.

What could Hiro have said to Sumiko to make her throw her flowers away? Celia wondered. She put her own flowers behind her back as she passed him.

Gran was home for lunch. When Celia gave her the flowers, she looked a little odd for a moment. Then she hugged her granddaughter and put the bouquet in a water glass in the center of the table. When Tani came in and saw it there, she burst into giggles and had to cover her face with her kimono sleeve.

Gran sighed and looked apologetically at Celia. " I was afraid of that. Honey, I do appreciate the flowers and I think they're very pretty. But you see, the Japanese buy these particular bouquets to leave at cemeteries as memorials. Tani-san thinks it's very funny that we're using them on the table."

When Stephen got home, he thought it was a good joke too. Celia didn't mind for herself, but this told her something about Sumiko. How difficult it must be to look Japanese, and have everyone expect you to be Japanese, when you didn't know half the customs and must be forever making mistakes!

Gran had spent part of the morning interviewing the head of a local department store to learn more about the trend these days in Japanese tastes, and she told them about that.

Celia explained about her meeting with Sumiko, and when she mentioned that Sumiko's grandfather was a famous artist named Gentaro Sato, Gran pricked up her ears.

" Mr. Sato sounds like someone I'd like to interview. Maybe we can arrange an introduction through your friend."

Celia shook her head doubtfully. "Sumiko says her grandfather doesn't like Americans. She went back home alone today, so he wouldn't know she had been talking to me."

"That sounds sneaky," Stephen said. "After all, Hiro came over openly to see us."

"It's different with Sumiko," Celia said, "because she's a girl. And in Japan —"

Stephen grinned. "In Japan they have the right idea!"

Gran was paying no attention to Stephen's banter. She sipped her coffee thoughtfully, with a faraway look in her eyes as if she were still trying to figure out a way to meet Mr. Sato.

"I'm happy that you've made a friend, Celia," Gran said. "But I don't quite like the idea of your seeing Sumiko away from the house if it's against her grandfather's wishes. Wait a little while on pushing this friendship, until we can find a solution. Now then — I've arranged to have my afternoon free, and I suggest that we three go downtown so you can get better acquainted with Kyoto. Also — you might as well start thinking about what sort of lessons you'd like to take."

"Lessons?" Stephen echoed in dismay. And Celia too looked at her grandmother in surprise. Surely they hadn't come all the way to Japan to spend their time in school!

The laugh wrinkles came out around Gran's eyes, and she tilted her head with its short, curly brown hair as she looked at them in amusement.

"Sorry I frightened you like that. But everyone who comes here starts taking some sort of lessons. It's part of the fun. Of course we take up things we couldn't possibly learn back in the States, and that gives us a better knowledge of Japan. You can take lessons in almost anything — the Japanese language, flower-arranging, samisen lessons. The samisen is the stringed instrument you may have heard someone playing after you went to bed last night."

Stephen made a face. "I can just see the kids at home if

I go back and play a samisen for them, or stick flowers in a vase."

"Give me time, dear," Gran said. "I hadn't come to boys' interests yet. I don't think there's anything sissy about judo, for instance."

"You mean I could take lessons in those trick holds the Japanese use, where they toss each other around?"

"I knew a boy your age in Tokyo who was doing just that," Gran said. "Anyway, you might think about these things and keep your eyes open for anything else that interests you. We can probably find a teacher for almost anything you want to learn."

After lunch they walked over to a busy street where taxis cruised, and took one of the tiny, beetlelike cabs downtown. On the way Gran asked the driver to stop at a small art shop. There she dismissed the cab.

"This is something for you to see," she told them. "And besides, it might help me in the matter of Sumiko's grandfather."

The sliding wooden door of the shop stood open, and Gran went through it, leading the way. Stephen, however, paused in the street, where a driver had just pulled up with a *bata-bata*.

"Hey, wait a minute," he called to Celia, who would have followed Gran into the shop. "Take a picture of me, will you?"

She turned back and watched while Stephen began to make gestures at the driver as he stepped out of the little three-wheeled truck. He motioned to his camera, to himself, and to the seat of the truck, and the driver got the idea, grinning widely. Stephen set the various complicated gadgets on the camera, checked the focus, and handed the camera to Celia. Then he got into the seat of the truck, while the driver stood watching in amusement.

"This will make a good picture to show the kids at home," Stephen said. "Everything's set — go ahead and snap me. But take it easy — that's the last shot on that roll."

It always made Celia a little nervous to take a picture with Stephen's fancy camera. She put the strap carefully around her neck, so she wouldn't have some horrible accident and drop the camera. Then she peered into the finder, while Stephen posed with his hands on the motorcycle handles.

Celia put a finger on the shutter and prepared to click. But at that crucial moment a passing cab honked its horn wildly and she jumped, knowing too late that she'd clicked the picture at the same instant. Stephen leaped out of the truck in annoyance. The *bata-bata* driver shook his head sympathetically, understanding what had happened, and went into a shop.

"Why couldn't you hold it still?" Stephen cried. "Now there's no more film till I change the roll."

"The — the horn scared me," Celia faltered, but she knew Stephen was disgusted with her. Silently she stepped into the shop, and Stephen followed, turning the film in his camera as he walked.

The entryway was a dirt floor, while the real floor of the shop was raised several feet and was covered by *tatami*. A man dressed in a dark kimono, with white *tabi* on his feet, came out and bowed low to Gran. She introduced him as Mr. Yamamoto, and he seemed to know her and be glad to see her again. Gran sat down on the edge of the *tatami* and invited Celia to a place beside her. She asked to see any prints he might have of the work of Gentaro Sato.

At the artist's name, Mr. Yamamoto made another low bow and disappeared into the shop's interior.

Stephen had stayed near the door, changing the roll in his camera. He finished just as the *bata-bata* went off down the street in a series of sputtering roars. He ran to the door and looked out.

" Well, I lost that chance," he said in disappointment as he came back to the shop.

" I'm sorry," Celia told him softly.

Stephen just looked at her. " Beauti — "

" Don't say that again! " Celia said, surprising herself by the sharpness of her tone.

" O.K., O.K.," Stephen shrugged. " Don't get so excited." Then he looked around the shop. " This doesn't look much like a store," he said.

Gran decided to overlook the sparks in the air and explained that in this sort of art shop the proprietor brought out treasures you might be interested in, showing you only a few things at a time.

There were no counters or showcases. The only decoration was a ceiling-high alcove on the far side, with a shelf upon which a beautiful pale-green bowl was set, with a few lotus flowers tastefully arranged in it. Above, against the wall of the alcove, was a long strip picture with an ivory cylinder at the bottom so it could be rolled up. Celia tried to concentrate on it so that the warmth around her eyelids would go away. She certainly didn't want to quarrel with Stephen in front of Gran.

The painting represented a mountainside with a few pine trees growing from it, and curling waves of the sea far below. It was quite simple, and Celia found it satisfying to the eye. She could imagine this as a picture one might like to live with happily for a long time.

Gran saw the direction of Celia's interest. " That *kake-mono* is undoubtedly the work of a famous artist. The alcove where it's hung is called the tokonoma and is considered dedicated to the presence of the household gods and the emperor. When you're in a Japanese house, never step into it, or lay anything there. It's the only place where pictures are ever hung."

Celia stole a glance at Stephen and saw that he looked bored and rather cross, but for once she didn't care, or at least tried to pretend she didn't.

In a few moments Mr. Yamamoto returned with several prints in his hand. He knelt on a cushion before them and held up one of the pictures for them to see.

"Gentaro Sato," he said, his tone revealing his respect.

In remarkably few strokes the artist had portrayed three tiny sparrows sitting on the graceful branch of a tree. One after another, Mr. Yamamoto held up charming drawings of a pine tree, a spray of cherry blossoms, a slope of mountain with a waterfall, explaining that Gentaro Sato painted only nature these days.

Celia nodded. "That's what Sumiko said. He's awfully good, isn't he?"

"Would you like one of these prints, Celia?" Gran asked. "For a *presento,* as we say in Japan. I won't offer you one, Stephen, since I know your interest lies elsewhere."

Poring over the prints, Celia felt enormously better. Mr. Yamamoto excused himself and went back to the inner room again. When he returned he carried a larger picture.

"Old-time style of Gentaro Sato," he said, and knelt to hold it before them.

This was not a print, but an original painting. At first glance, Celia felt a shock of surprise because the picture was so disturbingly different from the others. This picture revealed a more terrible kind of beauty. It portrayed a wounded Japanese warrior of feudal days dressed in battle array. He wore a padded, long-sleeved upper garment, and baggy knee-length pantaloons of some embroidered material. From his waist hung wide shields of armor, and on his head was a fantastic horned helmet with a protecting skirt that protruded outward over his shoulders.

"Wow!" Stephen said, taking some interest again. "That fellow's sure taking a beating."

The warrior had propped himself heavily with an outstretched hand against the trunk of a gnarled pine tree. From many places in his body shafts of arrows protruded, and his square shield lay upon the ground before him. In his right hand he held a sword, and though his enemies were not shown in the picture, you knew he faced them bravely in these last moments before he died. His mouth, indeed, his entire face was twisted in an agony of pain, yet you knew he strove bravely to hide what he felt.

The picture had been painted in somber shades of brown and pale tan, with the black of the pine tree and dashes of scarlet in the samurai's costume for accent. Celia gazed in fascination. Every austere line was beautiful and terrible at the same time. One had the feeling that the artist had felt something of this warrior's suffering in defeat.

Mr. Yamamoto explained that this had been painted many years ago when Gentaro Sato was in his youth, and it had won him great acclaim. The artist had earned his fame by painting scenes of Japan in the Tokugawa days when that family had ruled the country. The samurai in this picture was supposed to be an ancestor of Mr. Sato, and the sword he was holding came down from generation to generation through the family.

It was a long sword, Celia noted, with a tip that curved

slightly upward, the hilt hidden by the warrior's hand. She shivered and turned away from the picture, much preferring the quiet nature scenes with their gentle love of small growing things. Yet she had a feeling that this samurai in his death agonies would haunt her for a long time.

Mr. Yamamoto carried the picture away with reverent hands. It was clearly one of his treasures and not for sale. When he returned, Celia selected the Sato print of little winter sparrows, and the art dealer placed it between layers of cardboard and tied it up for her. She was very pleased with her *presento,* but she kept remembering the painting of the dying samurai.

6. The Cat That Mewed

THEY were only a short distance from the main shopping street, and they went out into the pale sunshine that bathed Kyoto, and crossed the Sanjo Bridge over the Kamo River.

Kawaramachi was a theater and shopping street, and while it was not so wide as the Ginza in Tokyo, it seemed very bustling and busy. Shops of all kinds, from the open-front type to those with show windows and doors, like any American shop, rimmed the sidewalks.

Celia paused before a window with a cry of pleasure, and Stephen stopped too — not because it was a doll shop, but because the doll in the main window was a samurai like the one they had just seen in Mr. Sato's painting. Now they could examine the minute details of dress and armor, and Stephen bent to study the little figure.

"The trouble with painting," he said, "is that the artist doesn't put everything in. Now if I took a photograph of this doll, you'd really get a record of what it's like."

"An artist doesn't have to put everything in," Celia told him heatedly. "He suggests, and your imagination does the rest. That is, if you have an imagination."

Stephen threw her a quick look. "Hey — you sound peeved. Why should you be mad? You're the one who spoiled the picture for me."

"Never mind," Celia said, with a glance at Gran, who was studying another part of the doll window. She always felt upset when Stephen was annoyed with her. And sometimes, for that very reason, she seemed to make things all the worse. But she didn't want Gran to notice the trouble between them. She gave her attention to the dolls in the window and tried to forget about her brother.

Some of the dolls were small, others a foot or so high, and the most elegant ones were dressed in fabulous silks and brocades — elaborate Japanese dress with handsome obis, or sashes, about their waists. The ladies had little black wigs upon their heads, combed in the intricate way that only the geishas — the entertainers — wore their hair. There was an old lady doll, and a little boy doll with the round plump cheeks she had seen on real children only that morning.

"They're so wonderful," Celia murmured.

"I know!" Gran said. "Why don't you make a Japanese doll for yourself, Celia? It would be something to remind you of Japan."

"Make one?" Celia echoed. "But I don't play with dolls any more."

"This isn't playing with dolls, Celia," Gran said. "In Japan, doll-making is an art. You can see that from these beautiful ones in the window. Many grown people have collections of which they are very proud."

"But how in the world would I go about it?" Celia wanted to know, as she now examined the dolls with more interest.

"When we get home we'll ask Tani-san if she knows anyone who teaches doll-making. I believe there are kits you can put together. How would you like lessons in that?"

Celia agreed in delight that she would.

Stephen shook his head over doll-making, but Gran only smiled at his expression.

"Never mind," she said. "We'll be polite and not tell you what we girls think of judo."

They went out along the street again, and Celia warmed to her grandmother with a little surge of affection.

When they came to the place where the street opened onto Shijo Bridge, Stephen recognized someone on ahead of them.

"There's that Japanese girl you were talking to this morning, Celia," he pointed out.

Celia saw Sumiko, with her two little girl cousins in hand, waiting for the traffic light to change. She called to her quickly, and Sumiko's dark eyes lighted with pleasure as she came through the crowd to join them. Gran was happy to meet her, and when she learned that Sumiko was taking her two small cousins into the Takashimaya Department Store, she suggested that they go along.

Inside, the store was like any busy American department store, except that all the customers were Japanese and you couldn't understand the language. There were escalators that only went up, and girls in maroon uniforms stood at the foot of each moving stairway, welcoming people to the store and telling them to be careful going up.

The floor that interested Celia most was the one where Western-style dresses for ladies were being shown. Dozens of plaster models, all exactly alike, were set so close together that they made practically a forest of blond ladies, each wearing a different dress, but all looking the same. How strange that the black-haired Japanese should like blond models!

On the top floor they stepped through doors onto an

open roof garden that had been given over to a play land for children. There were a small Ferris wheel, a tiny merry-go-round, trains that ran on tracks — all out in the open air, with a marvelous and complete view of the city all around.

"Most department stores in Japan have a play area on the roof," Gran said. "It's a nice custom."

Sumiko's little cousins were excited as she took them over to the train platform, bought tickets for a few yen, and tucked each one into a car. Off they went, clinging to their seats, solemnly enjoying themselves.

"Aren't they darlings?" Sumiko said. "But Joto makes me cross. The Japanese think a boy should never be corrected until he's at least seven years old, and even then he's given preference over his sisters and pushes them around just as he pleases. But he doesn't push me. This afternoon I slapped him good and hard."

Her eyes snapped as she spoke, and a spot of red came into each cheek. "Now I suppose I'll get another lecture from my grandfather for doing such a horrible thing."

There was a moment's awkward pause, and Gran changed the subject quietly.

"We saw some lovely paintings by your grandfather this afternoon, Sumiko."

Sumiko nodded without much interest. "He's always painting. That's his one pleasure, besides telling me that I must learn to be a proper Japanese." She waved as the two little girls went by on their train, but her thoughts were clearly on other matters.

Gran was considering her thoughtfully, and Celia hoped that Sumiko wasn't making a bad impression because of her discontent at home.

The silence grew long again, and to break it Celia spoke

of the samurai picture that was so different from Mr. Sato's
other work.

Sumiko glanced at her quickly. "You mean you saw the
painting of the samurai dying with his sword in his hand?
I'd like to see that one. I've heard that all the family were
upset when Grandfather gave that painting away. He'd
always refused to sell it — and then suddenly he wouldn't
have it in his house any longer."

"Why did he give it away?" Celia asked. "It seemed
like something fine enough to hang in a museum."

"I've heard it is," Sumiko said. "But when Japan lost
the war, Grandfather had a bad time. He went into a terrible depression after Hiro's father died so suddenly, and
sat looking at that picture for days at a time, they say.
Hiro was only a little boy then, but he still remembers.
Then one day Grandfather wrapped the picture up and
went out of the house with it and ordered that no one was
ever to mention it to him again."

"That's a rather sad story," Gran said. "It's hard for us
to understand Japanese thinking sometimes. I wonder,
Sumiko — do you suppose Gentaro Sato would be willing
to talk to me?"

Sumiko sighed. "I can ask him, if you like. But I don't
think he'll see you. He seems to dislike all the Americans
who come to live in that house you're occupying. I suppose he'd rather not see any Americans on our hill at all."

"Then don't ask him right away," Gran said. "In the
meantime, I wonder what he'd say if I wrote him a polite
note and asked if you might come and take lessons in doll-
making with Celia? She may need an interpreter, and it
would be a big help if he would let you come."

The gloom vanished from Sumiko's naturally pert face.
"That would be wonderful! Japanese dolls are beautiful.

But couldn't I just — just come? I mean, without asking Grandfather?"

"Sure, why not?" Stephen put in. "If Hiro comes, I don't see why you can't."

Gran shook her head firmly. "If Sumiko is going to make her home in Japan, she must be on good terms with her grandfather. And we must treat his wishes with respect, whether we like them or not. We're guests in Japan, and we mustn't forget it."

Sumiko looked so disappointed that Celia longed for some way in which to cheer her. "Never mind. If Gran writes him a note and asks politely, he may let you take lessons with me, after all."

"First," Gran said, "we'll have to locate a teacher."

Before they left the play-land roof, Celia stood for a moment at the parapet looking out at the great ranges of mountains that cupped Kyoto. Beside her, Gran pointed.

"Do you see that big bare space on that one mountain? That's where they build the big Daimonji bonfire every year. There are bonfires on other hills too. Perhaps you'll see them this summer. They come during the time of the summer festivals."

Sumiko and Celia looked at the huge space where all foliage had been kept from growing. Gran turned away to speak to Stephen, who was taking pictures of the two little girls, and Sumiko spoke softly to Celia.

"I wish we could skip those festivals. I wish they'd never come."

"But why?" Celia asked in surprise. "I should think they'd be beautiful and exciting."

"I suppose they are. But you don't know what it's like. Everyone expects me to do and say the right thing and keep all the customs straight, when half the time I don't know what's right and what's wrong. Hiro is always laughing at me."

"The way he did about those flowers?" Celia said. "But Tani-san laughed at me too, and I didn't mind."

"You're a foreigner and you look like one, so nobody expects you to know Japanses ways. But they expect me to, and it's a different sort of laughter when I make mistakes. You can't tell by looking at me that I'm a nisei — born in America."

On the way home that afternoon, Celia found her thoughts returning again and again to her new friend's difficult problem.

When they reached the Japanese house, Gran consulted Tani about a teacher for the doll-making lessons. Tani consulted Setsuko. Setsuko said she would run out and ask the people at the corner store. And off she went, slipping very quickly into her geta. The store was apparently a center for service and information of all kinds. The corner-store woman reported that she knew of a Mrs. Nomura — and she would fix. In a few days she would find them the most *ichiban* teacher of doll-making.

"*Ichiban*" was a word Celia liked. It meant the most A-number-one of anything.

Gran sat down to write a note to Mr. Gentaro Sato, and at the same time Celia started a letter to her parents. Already there were so many things to write about.

In the evening Hiro appeared to practice his English, and Gran asked him to deliver the note to his grandfather. She let him read it first — as further practice.

Knowing he was Sumiko's cousin, Celia looked at Hiro with even more interest than before. He didn't resemble Sumiko at all, and was completely Japanese in his manner.

He peered at the note through his round glasses and

read it slowly and carefully, needing help on only one or two words. But when he was done he looked unhappy and embarrassed.

" I am thinking my gran'father says no," he told them.

" Why should he? " Gran asked. "The war was over more than ten years ago. It seems to me the Japanese and Americans have become good friends since then."

Hiro groped for words. " My gran'father does not wish Japan to entering fight. But entering he does not think our country can be beat. Always the people believe that the gods will not be allowing Japan defeat."

Gran nodded thoughtfully. " I remember the legend. People thought the gods would always interfere and blow the ships of the enemy away from the sacred land of Japan. I suppose the same thing would hold for airplanes."

Hiro nodded. " Yes, this is true thing. When the gods fail Japan, my gran'father cannot accept this so terrible fate. My father is dying after war, when I am very small boy. So my gran'father after that paints only harmless birds and flowers."

" And he can't forgive America? " Gran asked. "Not even when we have forgiven his country and are anxious to be friends? "

Hiro made several apologetic bows. " Prease to excuse," he said, losing control of his " *l*'s " again. " Part of trubber is because you are coming to rive in this house."

"Trouble," Stephen said. " Live."

But Hiro's attention was fixed on Gran. " Maybe so you do not understand. This house belong to Sato famiry for many year."

" You mean your grandfather used to live here? " Celia asked in surprise. " You mean this is his house? "

"No more now," Hiro said sadly. "I am born here. And my father. Gentaro Sato also. This is fine house with big garden. But Occupation needs for Army famiry — fam-i-ly. After war we have no money. So we sell this house and go live in small house over there." Hiro gestured toward the house where all the Satos now lived crowded together. "I am bery sorry."

Gran smiled at him kindly. "You mustn't be. I can understand why he might resent those who came to live in his house. But if he never gets to know any Americans, it seems unfair that he should judge us. Anyway, Hiro, you give him that note. The Japanese are always polite and it may be hard for him to refuse. At least we'll try."

Stephen hurried to ask Hiro about judo lessons, and the Japanese boy was delighted to have the subject changed. There were very good classes in Kyoto, he said. He himself had studied judo for a while. He would be happy to take Stephen to the teacher and introduce him. Also, he had another project in mind.

"Maybe you like to see Japanese movies while making?" he suggested.

"You mean a movie studio?" Gran asked with interest.

Hiro nodded. "Uncle is working in movies. Studio here in Kyoto. I am happy to taking you."

They all agreed that it would be fun to go, and asked him to let them know the day and time. Hiro stayed for a while longer, talking to Stephen and letting him correct his English. Then he hurried home across the street.

Before she went to bed that night, Celia stood on the upstairs front veranda looking out over Kyoto just as she had done this morning. Now the mountains were dark shapes against the sky and a carpet of lights spread in all directions. The tooting of horns and the rush of traffic seemed more distant now, and the pale light of a misty moon bathed the city in an aura of mystery and glamour. Already she loved Kyoto, Celia thought, though she had made no more than a first step toward getting acquainted with it.

She went around to the rear veranda above the garden and stepped through the open shoji — a sliding door with paper panes — into her own room. Out in the middle of the floor Tani had laid out the padded *futon* that made up her bed. Celia got into her pajamas and slid between covers that were welcome in the cool breeze blowing down from the mountains. Near the head of her bed was a low standing lamp with an erect shade of white parchment, which sat like a little column on the mat and shed a soft yellow light in the room. With the honey-colored *tatami* and the beige wood of ceilings and posts, the room seemed glowing and golden in the lamplight.

She did not turn the light out at once, but lay waiting for Gran to look in on her and say good night. She felt much less homesick than she had felt the night before. Things had not gone very well between her and Stephen today, but at least Gran seemed less like a stranger every minute.

She heard Gran's slippers on the polished wood of the veranda, and turned her head. Gran was wearing her cotton *yukata*. She stepped out of the slippers and came across the *tatami*, imitating the pigeon-toed walk of a Japanese lady, so that Celia laughed softly.

"The only trouble," Gran said, "is that I can't get down on my knees as gracefully as Tani-san, or stay there as long."

She came down with a little thud and sat cross-legged, as no Japanese lady ever would. Then she made several little tucking pats around Celia.

" I spent a good many years doing this for your father, you know," she said. " It seems wonderful to have his children here in Japan with me. Good night, Celia dear."

When Gran had turned out the light and had gone to say good night to Stephen, Celia lay listening once more to the sounds of the garden and the street, as she had done the night before. The insect buzz seemed soothing now, and not at all strange. And she could identify the sound of geta, the strumming samisen, the horn of the tofu vendor. How quickly you became acquainted with a strange place and began to take it for granted!

Her thoughts went skipping about tonight, running over the happenings of the day. And all the time she knew perfectly well the thing that was waiting there to move into her mind and push all other thoughts away. She tried to hold it off, but it came in more quickly than she wanted it to. In her mind's eye she could see again all the terrible beauty of that samurai picture. She could see again the warrior's agony as he leaned weakly against the gnarled pine tree. She did not want to dream about that picture tonight, and she tried instead to remember the doll shop with its charming figures in silk and brocade. At length her eyes grew heavy and she fell asleep.

It was the distant mewing of a cat that broke through her dreams. She came suddenly awake and knew that it must be well past midnight. The moon was high now and its light shone on the satiny wood of the narrow veranda above the garden.

There it was again — the faint mewing. And Tani had said that only Neko-chan saw the ghost in the garden.

Strange, but in these night hours when nothing was the same as it was in the daytime, she did not feel in the least frightened. Nor did she feel that the little lady ghost who visited the garden was make-believe. In the moonlight anything was possible.

Softly she crept from beneath her quilts and crawled on hands and knees to the veranda. She did not stand, nor make any sound, but let her head come as high as the open rail, so she could peer beneath it and down into the shadowy space below. There was nothing there except fish pond and pine tree and lumpy bomb shelter. Nevertheless, she stayed very still, her breath held in waiting.

Something crouched in the shadows near the bamboo thicket. Something that was not wholly black, as were the shadows about it. Something with a face that shone hazy and pale in the moonlight as it stepped into the open.

She was glad she had the railing to clutch, for now she was more frightened than she had ever been in her life. Her palms on the polished wood were damp. This was not the gentle lady ghost of her fancy. The pale face had heavy black eyebrows, with deep eye hollows lost in shadow beneath. The mouth was a twisted black gash of suffering.

That much she could tell in the brief moment in which the figure was revealed to her. There was a nearby street light as well as the moon, and she saw the horned helmet, the flash of red in the garments. And there — there, surely, were arrows stabbing into a ghostly body.

Without a sound the figure seemed to drift across the garden, its tortured face uplifted to the moon.

Celia slid back from the rail and called softly to her brother. "Stephen! Stephen, come quickly!"

Hearing her, he rolled out of his own bed in alarm and came running onto the veranda. Celia covered her face with her hands.

"Out there! Out there in the garden!" she cried weakly.

Stephen stared in the direction in which she pointed. "What? Where? I don't see anything."

She opened her eyes and looked for herself. Moonlight lay shimmering in the still waters of the pond and made a silvery backdrop for the pine tree. But no figure moved in the garden. There was nothing there.

"You were having a dream," Stephen said, sounding justifiably impatient. "You'll be all right now. Go on back to bed." And he returned to his own room.

Celia shivered, standing there in her pajamas. For a few moments her eyes searched the garden in its every corner, but nothing stirred in the shadows. She crept back to bed and snuggled down beneath the covers. Had she really dreamed what she had seemed to see? Had her memory of that painting been so clear that she had imagined a samurai figure down there in the garden?

Somewhere in the depth of the house the ginger cat mewed again. The cat that was able to see a ghost.

7. Flaming Man

IN THE MORNING Celia was sure it must have been a dream. It had been fun to pretend about the lady ghost of her fancy. But this was something altogether different and she did not in the least want to believe in it. She hoped Stephen would say nothing about the matter to their grandmother, but she might have known he would never hold his tongue.

They were eating delicious Japanese melon for breakfast when Stephen looked at her and grinned.

"See any more ghosts last night?" he asked.

She kept still, eating her melon, drinking her milk. But Gran was interested at once.

"What's this all about?" she asked.

"It's a wonder she didn't wake you up too," Stephen said, "the way she yelled for me to come quick and look at the garden."

"I didn't yell," Celia objected. "I called you as softly as I could, and if you'd been a little quicker you might have seen it for yourself."

"What did you see?" he demanded. "I don't even know what I was supposed to look for."

"This sounds exciting," Gran said. "What *did* you see, Celia?"

"Maybe I was only dreaming," Celia murmured. She spooned a big piece of fruit and lifted it part way to her mouth. "I — I thought I saw someone down there in the garden." Then she popped the melon in and chewed rapidly so she couldn't talk.

Gran looked serious at once. "Someone in the garden? You mean an outsider? A man?"

Celia nodded, chewing.

Gran called Tani, who came running in from the kitchen. "Tani-san, are you sure you locked the gate last night before you went to bed?"

The maid vowed fervently that the gate had indeed been locked. She had seen to it with her own hands. Never, never would she take a chance that burglars might come in.

"I suppose if they really wanted to, they could come over the fence," Gran said. "But the Army put in regular doors downstairs, with locks on them, so I think we're all right inside."

"It wasn't a burglar," Celia said. "It was a — a —" she sought for the Japanese word, "an *o-bake*."

Stephen snorted, and Gran regarded her with interest.

"How do you know it was an *o-bake*?" she asked.

Celia threw a helpless glance at Stephen. "Well — it looked like that painting of a samurai that we saw yesterday. I mean, it had on a kind of helmet, and it wore those samurai pantaloons. And it seemed as though there were arrows sticking out of it. Though it could be I imagined those."

"I'll say you imagined!" Stephen laughed out loud. "I suppose this fellow was waving a sword at his enemies too, as he staggered around the garden."

"I didn't see any sword," Celia told him coldly, and

turned back to her grandmother. Now that she was into the story she might as well explain it exactly as it had happened. " The reason I didn't think it was a — a person, was because of the awful expression on its face. As if it were suffering terribly. If it had been a man in the garden and he felt as awful as he looked, he'd surely have been screaming for help."

" I see," Gran said gravely. She, at least, wasn't laughing.

Tani, who had listened intently to all this, had caught the word " *o-bake*." She nodded emphatically. "Neko-chan is crying last night. *O-bake* comes."

Stephen put a hand on each side of his head and rocked it back and forth in mock despair. " Now you've got Tani-san going too! "

The *neko*, hearing itself referred to, came wandering in from the kitchen to rub itself against Celia's ankle. She leaned down to stroke it, wishing it could come to her help and tell them what it had seen in the garden.

" I'm terribly disappointed that I missed all this," Gran said. " Next time we have visitors, do wake me up, Celia. I'm the one who wants to interview a ghost."

She left it at that, and Celia couldn't tell what she really thought. For that matter, Celia didn't know what she herself thought. The whole experience was too queer, and in broad daylight it didn't sound in the least reasonable, or possible.

After breakfast, while Gran was out in the kitchen telling Setsuko — as she did after each meal — how good the food had been, and they were exchanging complimentary bows, the little corner-store boy came in.

He chattered in Japanese to Tani, who explained that all had been arranged. Soon Mrs. Nomura would come to give Celia her first lesson in doll-making.

"Mrs. Nomura will probably feel more comfortable if she can sit on the floor," Gran said. "So you'd better have the lessons in your room, Celia. You have a low table there to work on, and you can keep your things in the cupboard right at hand."

All that morning Celia hoped that word would come from Mr. Sato permitting Sumiko to attend the lessons. But everything was quiet in the house across the way and she didn't catch so much as a glimpse of her friend. Someone else took the small children to nursery school, so Sumiko must be otherwise occupied.

Once, from upstairs, Celia saw Mr. Sato come out and stand at the rail of his own balcony. He stood for a moment studying the garden of his former home. Had Mr. Sato too seen the spirit last night, and was he too doubting the message of his own eyes? But there was no telling and he went inside shortly, without a glance in her direction.

Celia put away the book she'd been reading, wondering what to do with herself. Stephen had gone exploring again, but he had wanted to go alone. Gran sat at her desk in the living room downstairs, working at her portable typewriter. She mustn't be disturbed when she was working, and Setsuko and Tani were busy. Even the ginger cat had gone off on its own pursuits.

Celia went to kneel on the green silk cushion before the little lacquer dressing table and began idly pulling out the drawers again. They were filled with her own things now. Handkerchiefs, beads, a bottle of sweet-smelling Japanese cologne, and various small objects. Under a pile of handkerchiefs was the lacquer box with the pine tree on its lid. She took it out and looked at it once more. It might do to keep spools of thread in, or her scissors, pins, and needles.

But when she opened the box and put several spools of thread into it, she found that the cover wouldn't go on. She dumped the spools out and looked into the box. It was plainly more than two inches deep, yet it wouldn't hold a spool of thread because the wooden bottom was so shallow.

With one finger she poked at the bottom layer of wood and it seemed to teeter a little at one corner. Perhaps it was a false bottom and there would be more room in the box when she got it out. She turned the box over and shook it hard. The wedge of wood didn't fall out, but there was a slipping sound, as if there was something underneath, in the bottom of the box.

Now she was really interested. She managed to insert the blade of her small scissors, and in a moment she had the false bottom out of the box. Underneath were a few flat folded pieces of paper. She opened the largest one and examined it curiously. It was a narrow strip, about ten or more inches long and about five inches wide. The paper was a rough Japanese variety, and in the middle of it was a strange picture, printed in black ink.

The central figure was a barefooted man standing on what looked like a sawed-off tree stump. In his right hand he held an upright sword, and his brows were drawn down in an angry frown above eyes that looked very fierce. Behind him, rising to the top of the picture, terrible flames seemed to be raging. Celia couldn't tell whether or not his clothes were supposed to be on fire, but by his expression it certainly looked possible.

Below the central figure were two smaller human figures, also standing on sawed-off stumps. One, a man, had a bushy tuft of black hair on each side of his head and he was leaning on a staff. The opposite figure was a robed woman, her hands raised, palms together, in an attitude of prayer. Neither the man nor the woman seemed to be paying much attention to the flaming figure behind them. Beneath the whole was an oblong space in which Japanese characters had been written in a row.

Celia had no idea what the picture meant, or why anyone should hide it in a box with a false bottom. She laid it aside and picked up another folded strip of paper. This one was merely a wrapping to protect a small square of heavier white paper inside.

This bore a picture too, but one that had been carefully drawn in black ink, not printed. The drawing represented a tiny dragon, very intricate in detail, with every scale, every curve of its tail and of its open, fanged mouth beautifully worked out. It seemed to be looking back over its shoulder as if it saw something interesting behind it. Celia could well imagine that someone might want to save so exquisite a drawing as this.

As she started to put it down, she saw that the thickness of the paper had been misleading. There was another small drawing of the same size on a tiny square underneath. She separated the two and found that the second drawing was also of a dragon. Perhaps this was the one the first dragon was looking back to see. It was not a duplicate, but an individual picture of another tiny dragon, this one looking ahead. As much work had been spent on this drawing as on the first, yet all the details were different.

She laid the dragons aside and turned her attention to the last slip of paper. Again, the outer paper had been used for wrapping. Inside, cut out of cardboard, was a key a couple of inches long. But why of cardboard? What could you do with a cardboard key?

Still puzzling, Celia picked up the little box again and saw that something was stuck in the bottom of it. When she lifted it out carefully, she found that it was a dry, greenish-yellow leaf, almost like a small opened fan in shape. It looked familiar, as if she had seen the same sort of leaf on trees at home. But she didn't know what kind of tree it had come from. Why should anyone put a dried leaf in a box with these other things?

She replaced it in the box, put the two little dragon pictures and the cardboard key on top of it. For a moment longer she sat looking at the larger picture. Tani might be able to help her.

She went downstairs and found Tani outside sweeping the garden and washing down the steppingstones — something she did every day. Celia showed her the picture and asked her what it said underneath. Tani regarded it with interest.

"Paper comes from temple," she said. "Is picture of Fudo-myo. Very angry god. Is mad at all bad people. Very strong god for good people. Not afraid of fire. Not afraid of hurting."

"But why would someone save a picture like this?" she asked.

Tani tried to explain as best she could. This was a god who helped those who were suffering. That was his name written at the bottom. Someone in trouble might keep such a picture.

With that Celia had to be satisfied. She went thoughtfully back to her room and sat looking once more at the picture of the angry god. The paper from the temple looked yellow with age and the folds were brittle, as though it had been in the box for a long time. Forgotten, perhaps by the person who had put it there? Or perhaps tucked away by a child who was hiding his treasures for fun? But those dragons had not been drawn by a child. Once the artist Gentaro Sato had lived in this house. Did these things have anything to do with him? Celia wondered.

8. Under the Ginkgo Tree

THREE DAYS went by and still there was no word from Sumiko's grandfather. So far Mrs. Nomura hadn't come either, and when Celia asked about the lessons, Tani put her off with, "*Mada, mada*" — which meant not yet, or possibly never. It was useless to struggle with the phrase.

At least there were airmail letters from home, and Stephen was just as eager to hear from Mom and Dad as Celia was, though he was not so good about writing.

Once or twice Celia saw Sumiko from a distance, but she didn't dare wave to her or try to speak to her. One afternoon when school was out and Stephen was over near the shrine playing ball with Hiro, Celia wandered down the hill to watch the boys for a while. Carefully wrapped up in the pocket of her blue cotton dress were the two little dragon pictures — in the event that she might see Sumiko and show them to her.

Through Hiro, Stephen had gathered several Japanese students for friends, though he saw more of Hiro than of the others. He had forgotten his first notion that Hiro was an oddball and now counted on him as a best friend. Although these boys were all older than Stephen, they somehow seemed nearer his age. Sumiko, too, had seemed older than Japanese girls her own age. Perhaps one grew up faster in America.

Near the shrine a section of roadway had been blocked off by police so that traffic could not go through, and it was in this section that the boys liked to play ball. The shrines and temples seemed to be a part of the people's everyday life in Japan. While you had to take your shoes off if you went into the inner buildings of a temple, the grounds themselves were used as a convenient park. Often as she walked along the streets in late afternoon, Celia would see little girls bouncing rubber balls on the steps of one of the numerous little shrines which abounded in Kyoto. Or boys playing baseball inside the courtyards.

Today she walked along slowly, enjoying her growing feeling of familiarity with Kyoto. It was nice to know your way around in a new place. The old camphor tree up there on the hill, with two little girls playing house among its enormous roots, was now a friendly landmark. And the bright red decorations of some of the shrine buildings seemed to beckon to her cheerfully. Not even the sudden onslaught of the *bata-bata* scared her any more when they bore down with honking horns. She got out of the way, of course, but she no longer leaped like a frightened rabbit.

The only thing wrong was the lack of a friend to go around with. She didn't mind a certain amount of being alone. She could dream better by herself. But still — she wanted a friend. And Sumiko was the friend she wanted.

She felt rather proud of her brother as he made a difficult catch that won Hiro's delighted acclaim. She was proud, too, of his easy ability to make friends and of the way the Japanese boys seemed to like and accept him.

Nearby some little girls were jumping rope, and Celia saw that one of them had a baby tied to her back on a sort of cloth sling. As she jumped, the baby's head bobbed alarmingly, but no one seemed to mind — least of all the baby, who was sleeping through it all.

"Hello," said an American voice beside her, and Celia turned to find Sumiko and her two girl cousins watching her.

"Oh, but I'm glad to see you!" Celia cried. "I thought I'd never get to talk to you again. Did your grandfather say anything about the note Gran wrote to him?"

Sumiko shook her head. "I was right there when Hiro gave it to him. Hiro translated it into Japanese, and he listened to every word and didn't say anything at all. He just took the note back, folded it up, and put it away in his kimono sleeve. And he looked so stern that not even Hiro dared to ask him any questions."

"But won't he do anything about it?" Celia asked. "Mrs. Nomura is coming over — perhaps next week — and it would be so nice if you could be there too."

"I'll wait till Monday," Sumiko said. "Then I'll ask him myself. But my mother thinks he is sure to say no."

Kimi and Kiku, the two little girls, began to pull at Sumiko's skirt and plead for attention. She picked up a twig and bent to outline a hopscotch game in the dirt. Then she spoke to them in Japanese and each girl found a stone and began to play.

"That will keep them busy for a while," Sumiko said. "Let's sit down here on the bench where we can watch them and talk."

Celia had plenty to talk about and she sat down eagerly. "I've been dying to tell you," she said. "I think I saw the ghost, or whatever it is, that comes to the garden of our house."

Sumiko studied her uneasily for a moment. "If we were home in California, I'd laugh at you, but it doesn't seem so funny here. What sort of thing did you see? And when?"

Celia named the night and explained about the strange figure. Already it was fading a little in her mind because it was hard to go on believing in something like that. In memory the pale, agonized face grew more and more hazy, and it seemed increasingly possible that a trick had been played upon her by shadows and moonlight. Those arrows, for instance. It would have been easy to see pine branches thrusting upward and believe they were arrows when that samurai picture had been so sharp in her mind.

But Sumiko didn't question her story. She plucked a fallen green leaf idly from the ground and twirled it in her fingers.

"The next morning did you take a good look at the garden?" she asked. "I mean, did you check it for footprints, or a place that was trampled? Anything like that?"

"I never thought of it," Celia said. "Besides, Tani-san starts sweeping the garden so early that she would probably have removed anything that might be there."

Sumiko laughed softly to herself. "I don't suppose spirits leave footprints anyway. In fact, Japanese ghosts don't even have feet."

"Well, it wasn't a spirit, even though I did say so the next morning," Celia said firmly. "I just let myself get scared so that I saw things. I hate to think Stephen was right, but maybe this time he was."

"That was on Tuesday?" Sumiko asked, and gave her an odd, sidelong glance. "My grandfather saw something that night too. He mentioned it to my aunt, the mother of Kimi and Kiku. He truly believes that the ghost of his samurai ancestor appears in that garden. We can always tell when he thinks he has seen it, because he's keyed up and excited the next day. He stops painting and walks up and down in his room and around the verandas. He seems happy about seeing whatever he sees and he always has a better appetite and takes more interest in everything. But his daughter says he is a little worried too. He feels the spirit is trying to get some message through to him, and because he doesn't know what it wants, he is concerned."

During the last few days Celia had grown almost comfortable about that night, for she had come to believe the whole thing something that had grown from her imagination. But if Gentaro Sato had seen the thing too . . . !

"Don't look so startled," Sumiko said. "If anything really is coming to that garden on certain nights, I think it's only concerned with showing itself to my grandfather. So you needn't worry. Unless, of course, it decided it didn't like to be seen by you."

Sumiko twirled the leaf before her mouth and Celia saw she was hiding a smile.

"You're teasing me — " she began, and broke off to stare at the leaf in Sumiko's fingers. Then she looked up at the tall tree from which the leaf had come. Its branches pointed toward the sky, and all along them fanlike green leaves fluttered in the breeze. "Do you know what sort of tree this is?" Celia asked.

"Sure, it's a ginkgo," Sumiko said. "It grows back in the States too."

"Does it have any special meaning in Japan?" Celia went on. "I mean any sort of legend or story?"

Sumiko shook her head. "I don't know about that. There are probably sacred ginkgo trees here and there. Any terribly old tree seems to become sacred in Japan. They call this tree *icho,* which means duck foot. You can see why."

The fan shape did, indeed, look like the webbed foot of a duck. But none of this helped Celia. Why had a common ginkgo leaf been put in that box?

She reached into her pocket and touched the dragon drawings. "I have something I want to show you at home," she said in a low voice. "Some odd things I found in a small lacquer box. The box was in an old Japanese dresser that looks as though it might have been around since the days when your family lived there."

"What sort of things?"

Celia was just about to pull out the packet when Hiro came bounding over after a ball that had rolled their way. He picked it up and tossed it back to Stephen. Then he took off his glasses to polish them and spoke to Celia. Quickly she drew her hand from her pocket. She didn't want the boys laughing at her again.

"All is fix to visit movie studio pretty soon," Hiro said. "Is O.K. with you?"

"I'll have to ask my grandmother," Celia said. "I know she wants to go. Stephen can let you know."

Hiro was looking boyishly pleased. "I am being actor in movie. My elder uncle is arranging."

"He means he'll be an extra," Sumiko said lightly. "Though to watch him strut you'd think he was the star himself."

Hiro frowned at his American cousin. "You are knowing not anything," he told her.

"Have you ever been in a movie before?" Celia asked him. "Do you want to be an actor?"

He looked at her in surprise, his eyes serious behind the glasses. "No, I am not acting before. This is for fun, like you say. I do not wish to be actor. I will become *sensei*. Very important, very respected."

Sumiko seemed bent for some reason on taking him down. "Very respected, maybe. Teachers are always respected in Japan. But not very important — there are too many of them."

Hiro spoke to her curtly in Japanese, made a bow to Celia, and went back to the ball game.

"He says I am a stupid younger cousin and do not know anything," she explained to Celia. "But that's all right with me. I don't care what he thinks. All I want is to get back to America where I belong!"

She tossed the leaf aside and left the bench where they'd been sitting. Once more Celia felt sorry for her and wished she could find a way to help her. It seemed as though Sumiko was doomed to live an unhappy life unless she found some way to reconcile the two sides of herself — the American and the Japanese.

Apparently the ball game had broken up, for Stephen was approaching with another Japanese boy, and Hiro came with them. The little dragons would have to wait.

"Hi," Stephen said to Sumiko. "You look mad. What's happened?"

No one answered him. Stephen shrugged, and Hiro presented his friend Michio. This boy was as round-faced as some of the children, with the same rosy cheeks. He seemed a happy, lively sort of person and he stared at Celia's blond hair with unashamed interest.

"I've been telling Hiro about your seeing ghosts in the garden," Stephen said to his sister, his eye twinkling.

"You don't have to tell everybody," Celia protested.

"But Hiro's interested," Stephen went on. "He's on your side. Maybe the spirit *is* that old samurai ancestor of the Sato family, just as his grandfather thinks. I know, Hiro! Maybe you could come over to spend the night sometime and we could watch for it together."

Hiro looked startled, even a little frightened, Celia thought, but Sumiko didn't give him time to answer.

"That would be enough to scare any sensible ghost away," she said. "Besides, how would you know which night to pick?"

"For all we know, it comes every night," Stephen said. "If there really is something, I'd like to see it too. Hiro, could you come over and spend the night sometime soon? Then we could watch for it together."

Apparently these plans were moving too fast for Hiro's English. He looked at his friend Michio in concern, but the other boy's cheerful face showed no comprehension at all. He knew much less English than Hiro.

"Don't you get what I mean?" Stephen asked. "Look — if something comes at night to the garden, I want to see it. Maybe between us we could even nab it."

"Get it? Nab it?" Hiro repeated in bewilderment. "I do not understand."

"I mean catch it," Stephen explained. "Catch the ghost."

This time Hiro understood and shook his head. "But we cannot catch spirit. Is impossible."

"Sure, sure," said Stephen. "If it is a spirit. Probably there wasn't anything there in the first place. But if anything does come, I think it's human. Anyway, let's find out."

Hiro considered the matter thoughtfully, solemnly, while they all watched him. Then his face brightened and he nodded.

"I am enjoying to nab this ghost," he said.

Stephen grinned. "That's fine. If Gran is willing, we'll make a date with this samurai."

"Maybe it's not so funny," Sumiko said doubtfully. "If you go stirring up things that you don't understand, there may be trouble. This isn't America."

Stephen only laughed at her words. "It's all set," he announced. "We'll have an *o-bake* night and see what happens. You want to come too, Michio?"

But Hiro answered firmly for his friend. "Michio is outside of Sato family, outside Bronson family. Spirit will not like."

Sumiko smiled wryly. "Yes, for goodness' sake, keep this in the family, or all Kyoto will be laughing at you for trying to catch a ghost."

But as they walked away from the shrine grounds together, Celia thought that perhaps, as Sumiko had said, it really wasn't very funny. In fact, she didn't like the idea at all. But there wasn't a thing she could do to stop him, once Stephen was determined about something. If Gran gave her permission, there would probably be an *o-bake* night.

9. The Silent Scream

BY SUNDAY of that week there had still been no word
from Mr. Sato in answer to the note Gran had written
him. Gran seemed to think there was still time, but Celia
was growing less hopeful. Even if Sumiko asked him directly, he would probably say no, and she felt increasingly
disappointed. Here were these wonderful vacation days
slipping by, and there would be so much she and Sumiko
could do together. Yet because of one narrow, old-fashioned Japanese, they weren't allowed to be friends. It
didn't seem fair.

Sunday morning it rained and they went to church, blar-
ing their way through the downpour in a little taxi. But by
afternoon the weather cleared.

Stephen had met a couple of American boys who were
staying at the Miyako Hotel for a few days and he went
off with them to visit Nijo Castle that afternoon.

Celia, left alone, determined on a plan of her own. Several days ago, from the upstairs veranda, she had noted
what seemed to be a narrow path winding uphill through
trees back of the house. There should be a wonderful view
of Kyoto from the top of the hill. Since this morning's rain
it had turned warm and sunny, and she knew it would be
pleasant up there.

With Gran's permission, she started out right after lunch, taking along her sketchbook and some pencils and an eraser. She never felt lonely when she was drawing, and perhaps she could do a picture that would be good enough to send home to Dad and Mom.

Their house was last on this side of the street, and she turned uphill. Across the way the Satos' house looked secret and quiet behind its bamboo fence. Reed blinds hung across the upstairs rooms, and there was no one at all in sight.

Celia was recognized on the alley now, and a woman coming down the hill smiled and bowed in a friendly way. At the place where their own bamboo fence ended the alley ended too, turning into a second narrow alley that ran along the hillside behind the houses. Only a grassy path led upward from this, and Celia was almost at once in thick woods. In a few yards she came to a place where the path branched right and left, and there she hesitated, wondering which way to choose.

She was about to take the left-hand path, since it went up a steeper slope and looked as though it might go right to the top of the hill, when the queer feeling came over her that she was being watched. She would think nothing of meeting someone else walking through the woods this afternoon, but the feeling of being watched secretly was a little frightening.

She stood in the middle of the path and looked around carefully, her breath quickening. The woods were thick and dark, the air cool from the recent rain. Everywhere there were faint, dripping sounds as raindrops fell through the leaves. In spite of the sun overhead, it was still wet here beneath the trees. Ahead a twig cracked sharply, as if someone had stepped on it. That was too much. Celia turned to hurry back to the street and the safety of houses, when someone stepped right out into the path behind her.

She whirled to face him and then almost laughed in relief. It was only Hiro. He saw that he had given her a fright, and made rapid apologies in Japanese, telling her he was " so sorry " several times in English.

" It's all right," she said. " But why were you hiding? Why were you watching me from behind that tree? "

The boy's glasses made him look quite owlish as he stared at the tree that had hidden him. This time she laughed out loud in nervous relief because his expression was so funny. He looked as if the tree had behaved in a suspicious way and was to blame for shielding him. Then the meaning of her questions seemed to form into some Japanese thought in Hiro's mind and he smiled at her gravely.

" I do not hide for you, Ceria-san," he explained. " I am hiding for babies. Is game we play."

And sure enough, up from the end of the alley came the three smallest ones, Kimi, Kiku, and the little boy, Joto. They were all brandishing butterfly nets, and they rushed toward their older cousin with cries of delight. Joto immediately flung his net over Hiro's head, and Celia had to burst into laughter with the others.

The explanation was certainly a relief. Even though the watcher had been only Hiro, it had still given her an uneasy feeling to think that he had been, in a sense, spying on her. But now everything was all right.

The children had released their cousin and stopped their play to stare at Celia once more. Joto began to laugh and point his fingers at her. He said something to his sisters and they giggled in embarrassment. Celia was curious.

" What did he say about me? " she asked Hiro.

The older boy grinned as if he was amused also. " Joto is saying you have very funny eyes. Too big and round. Prease excuse — he is onry small boy."

Though she knew Hiro thought her a little funny too, she wasn't offended. It was interesting to realize that she looked as queer to the Japanese as the first Japanese face she'd ever seen had looked to her.

Already the children had forgotten her and were darting about, flapping their nets and shrieking excitedly. Whatever bugs or butterflies they were pursuing had plenty of time to get out of the way, but it was apparently all great fun.

"'Where is Sumiko?'" Celia asked.

Hiro looked a bit disapproving. " Sumiko takes lesson today in flower-arranging, like Japanese young lady. This she needs very much, Ceria-san." He knelt and gathered up a few twigs and leaves from the undergrowth and stuck them awkwardly together at the base of a pine tree. " Sumiko," he said, waving at the twigs.

" I see what you mean," Celia told him. Sumiko, clearly, was not very good at arranging flowers. " Flower-arranging should be fun."

" Sumiko does not like," Hiro said carelessly, looking with amusement at Joto, who was taking away a butterfly his sister had managed to capture.

Fortunately, the butterfly escaped in the scuffle, but Celia found herself wishing that Hiro had interfered in the interest of justice and democracy. She turned away from him and started up the steeper path. At once Hiro swung around in front of her.

" You are climbing hill? " he asked.

" Why, yes," Celia said. " There's no reason why I shouldn't, is there? "

Hiro gestured toward the second path. " Is better way. Is more pretty way, that side."

" But I want to go to the top," Celia protested.

" Other road goes to top. More better way."

She thought his insistence odd, but it didn't really matter. If she wanted to, she could come down the hill by the path he seemed to be guarding. So she smiled at him and went off on what she suspected was the long way around.

The butterfly chasers were quickly left behind as the path curved back gently above itself and wound uphill through thick woods of maple and pine and bamboo. Sun dappled the ground wherever it could make its way through the foliage, and birds chirped overhead. Around a turn the path steepened and she saw that Hiro was right — it did lead to the top. Around a bend she came upon a red gate, or torii, arching over the path.

The torii, at its simplest, was like two sticks placed upright with a bar across the top. But there were always decorative touches that made one torii style different from another. The presence of the red gate meant this was the road to a shrine. There would, Celia knew by now, be three torii altogether before the shrine was reached. Perhaps these gates were the reason why Hiro had indicated this as the better path. Yet it had seemed to her that he was almost relieved when she took his advice and turned away from the other one. No matter how she considered it, her encounter with Hiro still seemed strange.

The second torii appeared halfway up the hill, and the third was right at the top. The little shrine itself was like a dollhouse, with a slanting tiled roof upturned at the corners. Inside were elaborate, tiered decorations of red and gold, though, unlike a temple, the shrine had no image of a god. Two small stone lanterns flanked the building, and away from the shrine at a lookout point was a low bench of wood and concrete, where those who climbed the hill might rest and enjoy the view.

A red-leafed Japanese maple tree flung shade across one end of the bench and Celia decided that this would be a perfect place to sit and sketch. Now that she had reached the top of the small hill, she could see the mountains rising still higher behind, and stretching away on both sides in serrated ridges. Within their many extended arms lay the city, its sounds dissolved to no more than a hum in the distance. Only the booming of some great temple bell reached her, and its deep-throated sound seemed in keeping with this place and did not break the spell.

After days of mist, and sometimes rain, the sun felt warm and relaxing. She stood for a moment letting it bathe her lifted face with warmth. The peace of the mountains, the quiet of this lovely place, seemed to flow through her. From somewhere in the soft-wooded greenery of the mountainside came the liquid sound of bird notes, and she held her breath to hear the nightingale's song to the end.

If only she could capture something of this wonderful feeling in a drawing! A picture wasn't just something you saw — it was your feeling about it too. Perhaps that was the most important part of a picture — the feeling it brought to the one who beheld it, all because the artist had felt it first.

She sat down on the warm bench and looked about for the picture she would choose. Not a whole scene, but something simple and beautiful in itself — like that twisted pine tree on the hillside just below. She took out her pencil and began to block in the shape of the pine with its curved trunk and graceful outflung branches, the clustered needles that rounded the tree in graceful green layers.

No wonder Japanese prints always had a special look about them! They were just like the countryside they depicted. You would know the look of a Japanese pine tree anywhere, she thought.

How long she worked on, absorbed, with the little shrine behind her and the city below, she didn't know. Her drawing was taking shape now, and she was trying to get in something of the detail.

In her concentration she heard no step on the brown pine needles that covered the earth of the little clearing. She did not know anyone was near until she looked up, startled, to find that a man in a long gray kimono had come to stand beside her.

His bald head was well shaped, his face noble and keenly intelligent. Even as she gave a little start of astonishment, she realized that this was Sumiko's grandfather.

She remembered at once that he was a great artist, and she did not want him to see her poor little drawing. Quickly she flipped over the cover of the sketchbook, but he reached out and took it calmly from her hands. With the quiet, courteous manner of one who had the authority to do as he chose, he turned the pages of the book.

Celia could feel the warmth rise in her cheeks as he studied her drawing of Japanese children sitting on the ground painting, her sketch of a stone lantern, and one of that great camphor tree with the huge, uncovered roots. On one page she had tried to draw the head of little Kiku, and she saw him smile when he came to that. Then he turned back to the pine tree and studied it for a moment. With a gesture, as if he asked her permission, he sat beside her on the bench and held out his hand for her pencil.

She gave it to him wordlessly and watched while he

pointed to her drawing, then to the pine tree, and made
several swift strokes here and there on the paper. At once
the pictured tree seemed to take on something of the
beauty and life of the original and Celia could see where
lines were wrong, where she had missed the grace that was
there in the original.

Gratefully, she took the book back from his long-fingered
hands when he returned it to her. " It's beautiful now,"
she said softly of the drawing.

If he did not understand the words, he at least understood her tone, for he smiled again and nodded benignly.
Then he gestured toward the pine tree on the hillside below and spoke one of his few phrases of English.

" My teacher," he said.

She knew what he meant, and it was a wonderful
thought — that the pine tree itself had taught him out of
its own beauty. Celia forgot that he was Sumiko's stern
grandfather. She forgot everything except that this fine-
looking man was a great and distinguished artist. She
would have given anything to thank him, to ask him questions, to gain advice from him. But his language was not
her own and a wall stood between them. Nevertheless, it
was a wall that came only as high as their hearts, and over
it the old man and the young girl could look at each other
in appreciation and understanding. It did not seem to matter in the least that he was Japanese and she American, for
they had reached each other on common ground.

When he rose, he made her a low, very polite bow, and
then turned his attention to the shrine. Nearby was a stone
trough with water in it, and a tin dipper laid across the
stone. Gentaro Sato picked up the dipper and spilled water over his hands, then rinsed his mouth. Then he stepped
before the shrine, clapped his cleansed palms together

three times to attract the god's attention, and bent his head over his hands in prayer.

He didn't seem to mind that she watched him, and when he turned away he smiled at her gravely again, made her another courteous bow, and went homeward down the hill.

When he had gone, she sat on in a dream, thinking about what had happened, about this man who had once been famous all over Japan for his drawings of Tokugawa times and the days of samurai and feudalism. Yet he drew a pine tree so tenderly, so beautifully. She would not work again on the sketch in her book, because his pencil had touched it and she would treasure it always.

She still felt hushed and dreamy and spellbound when she started down the path again. After the bright sunshine of the hilltop, the woods seemed abruptly gloomy, their breath damp and chilling. A branch brushed raindrops against her face as she sought for the upper place where the paths separated so that she could take the other way down.

When she came to the spot, she nearly missed it because the second path was so overgrown with weeds, so little used. Perhaps that was because it was steeper and harder to climb. But going down shouldn't be hard, and she wanted to explore this path as well as the other one.

There were places where the reddish Kyoto earth had washed away, leaving stones exposed, and she had to scramble down steep banks, or leap over gullies. Hiro had undoubtedly been right in sending her the other way. There were no torii on this path, and as she descended, the woods seemed to grow increasingly thick and dark. She felt suddenly alone and hidden away, as if she were in a place where no one would ever find her if anything happened.

A sense of the eerie began to possess her. When she rounded a steep cut in the path and saw the black figures below her, she knew she was no longer alone in the woods. The chill of the damp shade seemed to seep to her very finger tips as she shrank into stillness.

A man stood in the little clearing below, his back toward her and one arm set akimbo. Just past him crouched two small black animals. Beyond the clearing the sun shone on a bright green world and it was that very brightness that made the figures in the woods seem so black.

For just an instant she thought them alive and waited for them to make some sound or movement. Then she saw that they were frozen there forever in the stone from which they had been carved. Nevertheless, there seemed to be something menacing and evil about them, and she stepped warily along the path, as if the stone man might turn and come toward her, brandishing the sword that he carried.

But the woods were utterly quiet; the figures did not stir as she tiptoed around in front to get a better look at them. Now she saw that there were four stone pieces in all and that shallow, crumbling stone steps led up to them. All the area grew thick with weeds and fern, as if no one had set foot in it for a long time. The nearest object now was a small stone lantern, not of the carved, symmetrical variety she had seen elsewhere, but roughhewn. It was no more than an upright column of stone, with the mushroom cap of another stone set upon it, and a still smaller stone upon that, to give the crude shape of a lantern.

Beyond, one on either side, were crouched two temple dogs, moss-grown and ancient, fiercely snarling, as if they guarded the approach to the stone man. The stone from which the main figure was carved had square box edges and from one side protruded the sharp angle of the crooked arm. One hand held an upright sword, its tip pointed skyward, and his rounded head wore a helmet of brightgreen moss. But the thing that compelled Celia's attention was the dreadful face that had been carved into the flat stone with a few simple lines.

The eyes were wide and staring, the nose was two flat lines, and below, the mouth opened in the terrible oval of a scream. The thing looked strangely human and yet frighteningly inhuman.

Back in the woods something rustled, and a wild, unreasoning panic filled Celia. She turned and fled down the stone steps and out into the sunshine, and it was as if the sound of that silent scream would follow her forever.

10. The Wagging Tongue
of Mrs. Nomura

IT WAS the following Thursday morning that Mrs. Nomura finally appeared with her doll-making equipment. In the meantime, Celia had visited one or two of Kyoto's beautiful gardens with Gran. Monday noon Stephen had come with them to have lunch in the dining room of the Miyako Hotel, where a terrace overlooked Kyoto on one side, and opened upon a fish-pond grotto on the other.

But during this time she saw nothing at all of Sumiko. Now, more than ever, she longed to see her new friend and tell her of meeting her grandfather on the hilltop, and of her queer discovery in the woods. She was curious about the little stone man, and about why he stood there in that lonely spot with his two snarling guardians.

When she had fled so foolishly from his presence that afternoon, she'd tripped over a tree root and gone sprawling. The ground was soft and she hadn't hurt herself, but the fall had given her a jolt and further frightened her. She had picked herself up and rushed out into the sunlight, to find that she was at the foot of the hill, near the lower branching of the two paths.

By that time Hiro and the children were gone, and she was able to brush herself off and quiet her trembling before she walked sedately back to the alley and her own gateway. She said nothing about her experience, even to Gran. It sounded so foolish, for one thing. And for another, the look on the face of the stone man still haunted her, as if he threatened her in some way, or tried to urge upon her something she did not understand. It was a secret she wanted to confide to Sumiko. Just as it was to Sumiko that she wanted to show the curious objects she had found in the lacquer box. Gran was sympathetic and she would be interested, but just the same she was a grownup and she would look at these things in a practical way that might easily brush the charm of mystery from them. It was more fun to have a secret that tantalized your imagination and could turn out to mean almost anything.

On Thursday morning something unexpected happened. Before the doll teacher arrived, Sumiko herself showed up at their door and Tani called for Celia to come downstairs. Sumiko's dark eyes were dancing and she wore a smile that had nothing of sadness in it.

"Will it still be all right if I come to the lesson?" she asked.

Celia stared at her openmouthed. "But your grandfather — ?"

"I don't know what got into him," Sumiko said. "But last night, when word got around — as it does about everything in the neighborhood — that Mrs. Nomura was coming to give you a lesson this morning, he just said calmly that I ought to go, and that I must convey his thanks to your grandmother for the invitation. He didn't give any reason, and I don't know what changed his mind. Of course, I didn't ask."

"I think your grandfather's wonderful," Celia said softly, and it was Sumiko's turn to look surprised.

Gran was out early that morning, so Celia took Sumiko

upstairs to her room, explaining about her meeting with
Gentaro Sato at the shrine. Sumiko gave a very American
whistle at the end of the story.

"How strange to have it happen that way! He must
have liked you, or he'd never have changed his mind."

"There are some other strange things I want to tell you
about," Celia said. "Maybe you can help me to figure
them out."

But before she could take out the lacquer box, Tani
brought Mrs. Nomura upstairs.

At first glance Celia was a little disappointed. Somehow
she had expected the teacher to look like one of her dolls,
to be young and dressed in a lovely, bright kimono. Mrs.
Nomura was old and wizened and a little stooped. Her
kimono was a drab dark brown, with a dull obi. Only her
eyes seemed bright and young, but they were so lost in
myriads of wrinkles seaming her face that when she closed
them they were hardly visible.

At once she went down on her knees on the *tatami* and
made each of the girls a low, ceremonial bow. Then she
looked up at them, bright eyes twinkling, and said, "Hi,
ladies."

Both girls burst out laughing and Mrs. Nomura looked
enormously pleased. "You like I speak English?" she said.
"Long time in Tokyo I have American frien's."

She had brought a *furoshiki* with her — the large square
of cloth that Japanese use to carry almost anything in. Now
she spread the big purple square out on the matting and
displayed its interesting contents. These were patterns and
pieces of colored silk and the dismembered sections of two
lady dolls. As she arranged these things to her satisfaction,
she talked to them volubly in her rather strange English.

Celia listened and watched, entranced, as Mrs. Nomura
moved her wrinkled hands lightly, tenderly, among the

beautiful silken materials, caressing a strip of embroidered gold brocade, picking up a bit of silk cord, tapping a small doll's head on the cheek affectionately. The girls were invited to select the heads they wished to use, and the kimono materials. Thin silk for the under kimono, something heavier for the top garment. Then patterns were spread out on the low table and the lesson began.

Everything must be done with fine, careful stitches and there must be no mistakes, no puckering, no crooked seams. Mrs. Nomura was cheerfully tyrannical about her demands and would plainly accept nothing less than her best from either girl. But you could tell that she was enjoying herself hugely.

She lived, she explained, in a house with a large family — not hers — and Celia gathered that they were all too busy to bother about her, or listen to her stories. So when she went out to give a lesson, she clearly made up for her silence by chattering. Especially when she found as attentive an audience as Celia and Sumiko.

From the storehouse of the *furoshiki* she took an ivory stick and showed the girls that the point of the stick would make a mark on silk. Thus they could indicate right on the goods how to duplicate the pattern.

There were certain things these geisha dolls could be doing and they must decide on that ahead of time. Mrs. Nomura would then provide each girl with the right kit. Celia chose to make a girl doing a fan dance, while Sumiko chose the hat dancer, representing a girl selling hats.

As they began the painstaking work of preparing material for the shears, Mrs. Nomura watched their every move with bright bird eyes and let her tongue wag as she watched.

Some surprising things came out in the two hours that she remained with them. Clearly she knew about the book

Gran was writing, and thought it a fine thing that an American woman wanted to write about Japan. And she seemed to know a great deal about Sumiko's family. She remembered Sumiko's father as a little boy, and Celia saw tears rise in her friend's eyes as the teacher spoke of him affectionately. But it was Gentaro Sato who seemed to interest the old woman most.

"Is very bad for him when Hiro's father die," she said. "Sato-san very sick inside." She pressed one wrinkled hand to her heart and shook her head sadly. "He knows here how bad thing is war."

"But I thought Hiro's father died after the war," Sumiko said. "He was a soldier, but he wasn't killed in the fighting. Though at the house no one will talk about his death except in whispers because it upsets my grandfather. Do you know what happened to him?"

Mrs. Nomura was perfectly willing to talk. She reached out to tap Celia's hand with her thimble and correct the direction her scissors were taking, and went right on.

Hiro's father, she said, had been severely wounded in the war, and had returned to Kyoto to recover. Before he could rejoin his company, the war came to an end. He knew that his captain was in Tokyo and he went, weak as he was, to be with him. His captain, sick at heart over the disgrace that had come upon Japan, felt that the only honorable thing to do was to kill himself. Many Japanese officers and soldiers had felt that way, Mrs. Nomura explained. Hiro's father would not let his captain die alone. He had died with him, going honorably to the gods by his own hand.

Mrs. Nomura shook her head sadly. "I have become Christian Japanese and I know this is bad thing to do. Is more better living so we give life to God."

Celia's scissors fell idle, for she was thinking of poor Mr. Sato, who had given his youngest son to America years before, and whose older son had been lost to him in this terrible way. No wonder he didn't like Americans — even if his feeling wasn't an altogether reasonable one.

"All Satos living in this house before war," Mrs. Nomura said, patting the *tatami* beside her cushion. "But after war, Sato-san is worry-worry-worry about old sword."

"What old sword?" Sumiko asked.

"Old sword long time in family."

"I think I know," Celia put in. "When we went to the art store last week and saw the picture Gentaro Sato had painted of his samurai ancestor, we saw a sword in the picture. The art dealer said it had been in the family for generations."

"*Hai*, this is so." Mrs. Nomura bowed her head in assent. "Hiro's father takes away sword, so enemy does not find. But Hiro's father goes to die in Tokyo, and sword is gone." Mrs. Nomura made a vanishing gesture in the air with both hands.

"It just disappeared?" Sumiko asked.

"No, does not disappear. I hear Sato-san gives order to son to destroy sword before son goes to Tokyo."

"But why did he do that?" Celia asked.

And Sumiko said, "Besides, if he did, then why would he worry about it now?"

Plainly Mrs. Nomura did not like to admit that she didn't know all the answers. She folded her lips together in a way that increased her myriad wrinkles and seemed to be thinking. After a long moment of intense concentration, she pushed her wrinkles into a smile of triumph.

"Is worrying for *menuki* on sword. *Menuki* very valuable. Maybe son does not destroy *menuki*."

This was clearly guesswork, and when Celia asked what *menuki* were, Mrs. Nomura gave up, her English inadequate to explain. Having thoroughly distracted her pupils, she suddenly became all business and would talk about nothing but the marvelous history of the Japanese doll. And she scolded them gently for thinking of other things. When her time was up, she left the work with the girls, gathered up her possessions in the purple *furoshiki*, made the knot that turned it into a bag, and bowed herself out of the house. She would come again this same day next week. In the meantime they must work hard.

When she had gone, Celia and Sumiko looked at each other with quickening interest.

"Do you suppose that's really true about the sword?" Celia asked.

"It probably is. Anyway, I'm glad to have all that family history explained. Nobody at home tells me anything. And of course my mother doesn't know all these things because she was in America until a month or so ago. Did you say you had something you wanted to show me?"

Celia got up and went to the little Japanese dresser. From the lower drawer she drew out the lacquer box with the gold pine tree on its cover.

"See what you think of these things," she said, and spread out the contents on the mat.

Sumiko nibbled thoughtfully at a strand of her pony tail as she studied the objects one by one: the ginkgo leaf, the temple picture of Fudo-myo, the tiny dragon drawings, and the cardboard key.

The key interested her and she picked it up. "Do you suppose this would match any key around this house?" she asked.

"What keys are there around a Japanese house?" Celia said. "There weren't any doors that locked until the Occupation people moved in and changed everything down-stairs. Now we have Yale locks and keys, and this isn't that sort of key."

Sumiko laid it aside and looked at the dragon pictures. "They're not the sort of work my grandfather does," she said. "He never works in miniature like this, using so much detail. He's famous for what he accomplishes with a few simple strokes."

"There was some detail work on the costume of the man in that samurai picture," Celia recalled. "I imagine that if he wanted to he could work like this."

Sumiko flipped her black pony tail out of the way and snapped her fingers. "I know! Why don't you bring these pictures over to my grandfather and show them to him?"

"Oh, no!" Celia shook her head in dismay. It was one thing to meet Gentaro Sato, the artist, on the hilltop, when they had needed no words between them, and quite something else to intrude upon Mr. Sato, the stern grandfather, in his own home where she couldn't talk to him at all. "Why couldn't you show them to him yourself?" she added.

"I won't show him anything," Sumiko said, frowning. "He doesn't approve of me."

An uncomfortable silence fell between them. To break it, Celia started to tell Sumiko about the stone man in the woods, but she had hardly begun when Stephen came home from his judo lesson. They heard the floor of the veranda creak as he came along it and he paused to look in at them through the open shoji.

"This veranda's just like the 'nightingale floor' at Nijo Castle," he said. "They've got a whole wide corridor there that squeaks when you walk on it. The guide said it was built that way so the daimios — the lords — would know if an enemy tried to sneak up on them. They say it doesn't squeak if you walk on it properly, but only if you tiptoe guiltily. It sure squeaked for us!"

While he was speaking, Celia reached quietly for the mysteries to put them away, but she wasn't quick enough. His eye had fallen on the picture of the flaming god.

"What's that?" he asked, and stepped out of his slippers to cross the *tatami* in his socks and pick up the picture.

Celia wished she had gotten it out of sight in time. "It's just a picture I found with some stuff in my dresser," she said carelessly. "Tani-san says it's of a god who helps people who are suffering to be strong."

"He sure is suffering!" Stephen dropped the picture and knelt to look at the other things. The tiny dragons did not particularly interest him, and he scarcely glanced at the leaf, but the carboard key caught his attention. "What's this for?"

"I don't know why anyone would make a key out of cardboard," Celia said.

"It looks like the tracing of a real key," Sumiko suggested. "But what could it be for?"

Stephen turned it over in his hand a few times and then went out on the narrow veranda to stare down into the garden. "Could be it's a pattern of the bomb shelter key. I think it's about the right size. But what's the point in making a picture of a key?"

"Could a real key be made from it?" Celia asked.

"Of course not. You'd have to know the thickness too. This only gives length and shape. Oh, well — the Japanese are always doing funny things. Say — don't forget — we're going to that movie studio next week. You coming, Sumiko?"

Sumiko shrugged. "I suppose it depends on my grandfather. Since it's a relative who has asked us, maybe he won't mind."

Celia put the articles away again in the lacquer box. It occurred to her that she might take those dragons along once more when they went to the studio. Perhaps they would meet someone she could ask about them. If not there, then somewhere else. They had to mean something.

11. Sword of a Samurai

By THE TIME the day of the trip to the studio rolled around, Celia's Japanese doll was beginning to take shape. But the mysteries had moved no nearer solution than before.

Gran was especially delighted about this studio trip. Some Japanese movies, she told Stephen and Celia, were very fine and had won acclaim all over the world — though most Japanese liked American movies better. On the other hand, the B pictures were sometimes quite funny, and if that was what they were filming during this visit, it was possible to see some real action. Anyway, she hoped to get some general material for her book.

Celia, too, looked forward to the trip. The flight bag had at length arrived from Tokyo, with everything in it intact. And now that Stephen had his precious light meter back, he was in a much better humor. His annoyance with his sister had died away, and Celia hoped nothing would happen to start it up again.

Since Hiro was to be an extra in a movie, he went ahead to the studio early that morning, and his friend Michio went with him. But he had left passes for the others, supplied by his uncle, and Sumiko turned up happily on their doorstep just as Gran, Stephen, and Celia were putting their shoes on.

They caught a cruising taxi for the trip across Kyoto. The morning was hot and muggy, with the sun shining through a thin haze. Gran and Sumiko talked for most of the trip across town, while Stephen watched the passing scene and Celia dreamed and thought her own thoughts. Once or twice she felt in her pocket to make sure the envelope with the dragon drawings was safely there.

Last week, after Stephen had said that the cardboard key might represent the one to the bomb shelter, Celia had gone outside when no one was watching and examined the lock. It did, indeed, look as though it might be the right size and shape for that key. But she was no wiser than before as to why anyone should have cut out a picture of a key.

On the way back to the house, she had asked Tani where the key to the shelter was kept. But neither she nor Setsuko knew. The American families had never opened the shelter and no one had bothered about the key for a long, long time. Certainly it wasn't around the house with any of the other keys. Yet Celia's feeling that the key might lead to something more than just a door increased in spite of discouragement.

When the driver pulled up in front of a wide gate, they were all glad to get out and stretch their legs. Gran showed their passes and they walked through the gate into the sprawling grounds of the studio. Apparently, they could wander around as they liked, and by following their noses would probably come to something interesting.

Inside it was dusty, and there were small stones that got into their shoes. Stephen investigated a few large, shed-like buildings as they went by, but reported that while there seemed to be sets inside, everything was dark and deserted. He had his camera along, of course, and was hoping to get some good shots of movie-making.

A growing clamor rose behind them as they walked along, and they turned to see that a tour group of some fifty or more Japanese was streaming through the entrance gate. A neat, efficient-looking Japanese girl in a blue uniform hurried them along at a good rate and seemed to know just where she was going.

"Let's follow them," Gran said. "Tours are a big thing in Japan. Sometimes, when I visit a temple or some place like this, I think half the country must be on tour."

Their own group kept a discreet distance from the tour, but followed as it twisted like a long, colorful snake among the sheds and replicas of scenes. Here and there Celia saw architecture that looked familiar and realized that replicas had been built of a number of famous Kyoto buildings.

The entire place still seemed deserted, as if all the inhabitants of this make-believe world were off on a holiday. Stephen had Gran and Sumiko and Celia pose for a picture in a wooden gateway that was real only on one side, and then they wandered on, still following the tour.

Rounding the corner of a tumble-down shed, they ran without warning into a scene of action. A mob of a hundred or more extras, men and women dressed as Japanese peasants of a bygone day, were gathered in a large open area. Some of them wore straw hats fastened under their chins; some wore varieties of coolie coats, patched trousers, or kimonos tied high above their bare legs. Some of the women had material of a dark color over their heads in the manner of a hood, while some of the men had sweatbands of cloth bound about their foreheads. Streaks of brownish make-up marked the faces of many of the actors, and most of the mob carried staves or sticks, or even long knives. Almost anything seemed to go in the way of costume and equipment.

The tour guide led her obedient sheep to the far side of the crowd, where they wouldn't get in the way of the camera, but Gran said she thought their own small group would be all right here with this small shed to hide them. The only trouble was that the principal actors and what they were doing were completely out of sight in the direction of a high gate toward which the large peasant group faced. The actors seemed to be up on a platform before the gate, and once in a while you could see the top of a head, and hear their distant voices, but not much else.

Sudden words over a loud-speaker alerted the extras. They all leaped up, raised their sticks and knives threateningly, and shouted. Stephen snapped a quick shot with his camera. Then everyone returned to dozing, or to private conversations. There were too many extras to locate Hiro, and he and Michio were nowhere in sight.

Gran found some wooden steps that were part of an old set and sat down beside a fierce-looking fellow who appeared to be a bandit. It developed that he had lived in New York City for several years and spoke English.

Stephen was growing restless. "Do you suppose this is all we'll get to see? I wanted to get a shot of a real samurai fight. In a movie I saw with Hiro they sure whacked at each other. Nobody really got hit and it was pretty funny, but it would make a good picture."

"Maybe you could climb around through those shacks behind us and get to a place where you can see," Sumiko suggested.

Stephen looked in the direction she indicated. "Good idea. You girls stay here and I'll go see what I can find."

"Let's go too," Celia said to Sumiko, and they started off on Stephen's heels. He looked back at them and shook his head, but Celia pretended not to see.

"Don't pay any attention," she said to Sumiko, and they

went right on. It wasn't fair of Stephen to have all the fun and shut them out.

They had to climb over the logs of something that looked like an old stockade, squeeze between ripped canvas sides of scenery, run up steps that went nowhere and jump down the other side. But the exploration was fun, and they could tell by the sounds that they were getting closer to the real action. Now one of the actors was shouting his lines furiously in Japanese, while someone else answered him angrily. Stephen had gone out of sight into a sort of cottage with a thatched roof and the girls followed him.

There was the usual platform floor inside, though no *tatami* had been used here. Stephen was leaning out a rickety window, and by creeping up behind him they could see what was happening.

Outside, huge lamps had been set up to throw brilliant light on the scene. Glass reflectors, six feet or more across, stood in frames where they could catch the light and throw it back upon the scene to increase the brilliance. Several persons sat about in canvas chairs, and a man with a megaphone, white riding pants, and leather puttees, like an old-fashioned Hollywood director, stood up shouting orders at the actors. A script girl was at his side, pages of Japanese characters in hand, while make-up people ran about, arranging a lock of hair here, the fold of a kimono there.

The center of all this activity and attention was a handful of actors in full costume. Three delicate Japanese ladies in beautiful kimonos of magenta and peach and blue hovered about the fierce figure of a samurai in helmet and baggy pantaloons.

At a signal, make-up people leaped back, the script girl

fluttered her pages, the director gave an order, and the camera began to grind. The samurai drew his sword with a great shout of anger, while the ladies shrank behind him in a show of alarm. As the samurai advanced, the leader of the peasant farmers turned and shouted to the mob behind him. They all shouted back and waved their sticks and knives in the air.

It was very exciting, and Celia leaned farther out the window beside Sumiko and Stephen so she could see better. They were really close now, with the director and his assistants almost below them — though fortunately no one had looked around to notice their presence.

Now the samurai stepped forward, forcing the peasant leader back at the point of his sword, and once more he shouted threateningly in Japanese. This time his words must have alarmed the peasant mob, for the whole great throng groaned and cringed backward, like a wheat field over which a strong wind had blown.

In her excitement, Celia leaned still a little farther, and suddenly the flimsy structure of the window frame gave way with a splintering crash and all three were catapulted through space to the ground, landing practically behind the chair of the director.

The man leaped up as though he had been prodded with a sword, and turned around. The cameras stopped grinding, the actors paused in what they were doing, the extras gaped, and it seemed to Celia, her face blazing, that there must be several hundred people staring at them, for they had practically tumbled into the movie.

Stephen was on his feet first, dusting himself off and regarding Celia in despair.

Sumiko had jumped up too, and pulled Celia after her. By the stinging of one knee, Celia knew she had bruised and skinned it, and her hand felt as though there might be a big splinter stuck in the skin. But she dismissed the sting of pain for other matters more important.

The director came over, and although he didn't approve, his questions were courteous. Sumiko bowed repeatedly in her best Japanese manner and tried to apologize and answer him.

"What's he saying?" Stephen asked. "Tell him it was an accident. Tell him my sister — "

But no one paid any attention, least of all Sumiko, who was trying to explain the unexplainable to the group that had gathered around to see what had happened. The samurai actor on the platform leaped gracefully to the earth and came over to them, his sword still in hand. He looked fiercer than ever close up, with his exaggerated make-up and his eyebrows curling up at the outer corners in a black line.

But he flashed the unexpected guests a smile and said, politely, "Please, what is happening?"

The director would have spoken, but Stephen, happy to find someone who understood English, began explaining again about his sister and how she had leaned too far out the window, and how they had all fallen through. The samurai laughed out loud, back on the platform the pretty young ladies began to giggle, and the peasant leader smiled from ear to ear. Celia suspected that the director was not amused, but with true Japanese courtesy, he hid his irritation.

"The actor is Hiro's uncle," Sumiko whispered to Celia. "He's explaining that it's really all his fault, as he invited us here, and after all, if no care had been taken to get us a place where we could see, we were not to blame. He is making it sound like a joke, so maybe it will be all right."

Finally one of the assistants ran off to get a couple of boxes and a board to lay across them, so that a rude bench was set up at a place behind the director where they could all see very well indeed. The director bowed them to the bench, making them the guests of the studio in a very grand way. At once everyone began bowing to everyone else and Celia found that she and Stephen and Sumiko were all bowing as hard as the others. Bowing was something you picked up very quickly in Japan.

The samurai bowed too, then winked at them in American fashion and went back to the platform. Everyone settled down and the scene was shot over again, without any dramatic interruptions or sound effects toward the end.

Nevertheless, Celia discovered, taking time now to remove the splinter from her hand and examine her knee, movie-making could be a very slow process. Mostly the extras sat around for minutes on end and did nothing at all. The actors on the platform rehearsed a scene in various ways and then a portion of it was shot — only to be taken over again, if the director was not satisfied. She hoped to goodness that Gran wasn't worried and looking for them. Stephen had managed to get a couple of shots he wanted, and was happy again.

Celia couldn't blame Stephen for thinking her a dumb bunny. One of these days she would just have to show him that she was smarter than he thought.

At last a break came in the movie work. The extras were dismissed and the crowd began to break up. Once more Hiro's uncle leaped from the platform and started back to them, still carrying his sword. With one hand he unstrapped the elaborate helmet with its skirt that protruded over his shoulders, and threw it off, revealing the samurai haircut he wore underneath. A long lock of hair had been

caught at the top of his head like a short pony tail and
skewered in place with a decorative pin. He handed the
helmet to one of the make-up girls and came toward them,
smiling.

Hiro had apparently told him all about them, because
he knew their names and spoke to each in turn. He seemed
especially interested in Sumiko, whom he had not met
before.

"You are Hiro's new cousin just come from America,
yes?" he said. "Before war I have lived long time in California, so I speak American pretty good."

He was about to sheathe his long sword, but Stephen
held out his hands. "Please, will you let me see it, sir? I've
never had a look at a samurai sword before."

Proudly the actor held out his sword. "This is good one.
Very old. Not imitation for play. Samurai takes much care
of sword because it means his life. In old days of Tokugawa reign, Japanese sword is work of art."

Celia, pressing close as she dared so that she could examine the sword too, saw what he meant. The handsomely
decorated hilt was almost hidden by strands of silk and
strong fiber, wound back and forth crisscross, so that only
small diamond-shaped portions of the sword hilt were left
exposed. In these spaces were set tiny ornaments of gold
and silver and bronze. The circular guard which divided
the hilt from the blade was a miniature picture in open
metal work, with bamboo leaf patterns in the design.

"Could be samurai has three swords total," the actor
said, and showed them another, shorter sword which he
wore with the hilt protruding behind his waist. "Small one
is called *tanto* and is samurai's best friend. Never it leaves
his side, though other swords must be removed before entering house of friend. With this sword, if honor so de-

mands, he will take his own life."

Celia shivered, remembering Hiro's father. But of course Hiro's father had not been a samurai. All this belonged to the distant past.

"What's the third sword?" Stephen asked.

The actor shook his head regretfully. "I cannot show you here. But you will find still treasured in some families and in our museums. That is the *tachi*. Very high, important samurai used this sword for special ceremonial occasions. This one is handed down through family and much treasured. Before war Gentaro Sato owned such a sword."

Hiro's uncle held his own sword out by the blade for Stephen's inspection, and Celia and Sumiko looked closely too.

"Blade is no more sharp," the actor said, laughing. "Is no good if I cut off pieces of other actors by mistake."

A small golden object on the sword hilt caught Celia's eye and she bent to examine it more carefully. Beautifully wrought in gold and bronze and fastened to the hilt was a tiny goose with its wings outspread, flying. She touched it lightly with her finger.

"Did they always decorate the swords like this?" she asked.

"*So desu* — yes, of course." The actor was pleased. "You have found the *menuki*. "See —" he turned the sword over and showed her the other side of the hilt. "Here is flying goose this side also. But different from the first one. *Menuki* means the fist place, and such ornaments, all individual, never alike, were placed on hilts of all swords to give fighter good grip on his sword."

Sure enough, the lovely gold and bronze goose on the other side was an individual in its own right. Its wings and legs were different, and so were the tiny feather markings. Celia remembered the little dragon pictures, which were also of carefully drawn individual beasts. She felt in her pocket and drew out the envelope that contained them.

"Do you think these could be drawings of – of *menuki?*" she asked.

The actor looked at the drawings carefully, his fiercely drawn eyebrows, which were not in keeping with his friendly manner, seeming to scowl.

"Yes – looks like *menuki* picture. Is possible, I think."

Celia glanced at Sumiko and put the tiny drawings back in the envelope. Stephen was paying no attention, for he had spotted Hiro and Michio in the dispersing mob of extras. The two were coming toward them, Michio in his student's clothes and visored cap, Hiro in the short trousers and dark coat of the peasant costume, a sweatband of blue cloth tied about his head.

While Stephen told the boys what had happened, Celia put the envelope away in her pocket. As Hiro listened, he threw a disapproving look at Sumiko, and when Stephen finished, he spoke to her in Japanese. Sumiko shrugged and turned away from him indifferently.

"He's always telling me I don't know Japanese customs and courtesy. He thinks I should have kept you from coming so close."

When they'd thanked Hiro's uncle and said good-by they crossed the now empty field, looking for Gran. She was still sitting on the steps where they had left her, busily writing in her notebook. To Celia's relief, she looked up and smiled when she saw them coming toward her, and didn't seem in the least perturbed.

"Hello, there! So you and Hiro found each other. I thought I'd better stay in one spot until you came back.

Besides, I had a lot of things to put down in my note-book. I hope you saw more of what was going on than I did. A little while ago there was some sort of big commotion up in front, but I couldn't find out what had happened."

The girls began to laugh and it was Stephen who explained. " Celia fell through a window," he said — which wasn't entirely correct, since Stephen had fallen through too.

She and Sumiko had another thing in common, Celia thought. Sumiko had a cousin and she had a brother who often disapproved and thought they weren't very bright. Somehow it didn't seem quite so hard to take when she knew she had company.

12. An Empty Scabbard

SUMIKO was still not permitted to run in and out of the Bronson house as much as Celia would have liked her to. But the doll lessons progressed, and afterward Sumiko always stayed a little longer than was necessary. But there was no invitation issued in return to either Celia or Stephen to visit the Satos' house.

Gran said that was partly because so many Japanese lived under crowded circumstances. There were a lot of people living under the Sato roof. Japanese houses were not built for much visiting back and forth. A Japanese might invite you to his house for some ceremonial purpose such as moon-viewing in September, or to see a beautiful garden or a rare treasure, but usually there had to be a special reason.

Thus it came as a surprise when Sumiko ran over one morning and asked Celia if she would come to see her grandfather. His daughter had taken the small children out, and only her mother and Hiro's mother were home just now.

"He wants you to come," Sumiko added, "though I really don't know what's up."

Celia was both pleased and a little dismayed. She was not at all sure she could recapture the way she had felt about Gentaro Sato that day on the hilltop. She had dropped back again into feeling a little awed and frightened by him. Still, she wouldn't miss going, and Sumiko would be right there to translate, so it might be possible this time to talk to him a little.

"Bring the dragons," Sumiko whispered, when Celia was ready to go.

Celia hesitated for a moment and then went to get them from the lacquer box.

As they went through the living room, where Gran sat at her typewriter, she looked at them through her blue-rimmed glasses. "Don't forget that I'm dying to have an interview with Gentaro Sato. If the right opportunity should offer, do mention my book to him, girls."

They ran across the alley together and Sumiko's mother met them at the gate of the house. She was a small woman, rather sadly pretty and not very old-looking. Sumiko said her grandfather insisted on all the grown women in his house wearing the kimono, so her mother had discarded Western dress to please him.

"But not me," Sumiko whispered, patting her American plaid skirt affectionately. "I'd feel silly in a kimono and I'd never be able to walk with those little pigeon-toed steps the Japanese women use. But if you go walking naturally in a kimono, it flaps open."

The Sato house was far smaller than the one they had formerly owned, and it held a good many people. Sumiko's mother, Hiro's mother, Mr. Sato's daughter and her three small children, plus of course Hiro and Sumiko, all lived in the downstairs rooms. Fortunately, in a Japanese house the *futon* beds were folded away in cupboards in the daytime and there was very little furniture.

Only a section of the house had an upstairs, and this

part was reserved for Gentaro Sato. Sumiko's mother had work to do in the kitchen, so it was Hiro's mother who went upstairs with them. She smiled delightedly at Celia and murmured a welcome in Japanese. But she too was clearly in awe of her father-in-law, for her smiles vanished when she ran upstairs ahead of them to see if Mr. Sato was ready to receive company.

The usual slippers had been provided at the doorstep, so that Celia could take off her shoes and walk on the polished floors of the entryway and stairs. By now she had learned caution in climbing the steep, slippery stairs with their narrow steps that were best suited to small Japanese feet. She and Sumiko padded up, left their slippers at the head of the stairs, and stepped onto the springy, wheat-colored *tatami*.

The sliding fusuma in this upstairs section had all been opened to make one large, airy room, open on three sides, looking out on hillside and city. This was the artist's studio. Gentaro Sato came to greet them, and Celia saw that he wore a fine silk kimono of charcoal gray, with a small crest in white on each sleeve. He bowed courteously low, and Celia found herself bowing too and murmuring, " *O-hayo gozaimasu* " — the polite " good morning " Gran had taught her.

Mr. Sato gestured with a paper fan and led them away from the stairway to a place where cushions of purple silk had been set out for their coming. Sumiko and Celia curled up on two of the cushions, while Mrs. Sato took one placed a little farther back from the others. The artist knelt on a cushion before a large black lacquer tray on which stood painting things.

Among them were a lovely blue jar containing many brushes with bamboo handles, some dishes of water, and

tubes and saucers of paint. Beside him rose a tiered set of
many drawers with small brass handles. Here he probably
kept sheets of paper and various other equipment con-
nected with his work.

It was odd, Celia thought, but Mr. Sato did not look at
all strange with his finely shaped bald head. In fact, it
gave him a rather noble appearance, and one of great in-
telligence. While his face looked as though it might grow
stern on occasion, his expression was most benevolent this
morning, his smile kindly. Before he spoke to them, he
gave Mrs. Sato a glance, and she bowed and hurried off
for the tea that was always offered a visitor. Then he
opened a drawer beside him and took out two small fans
which he presented with ceremonious gestures to Celia
and Sumiko. Sumiko looked impressed and pleased, and
said quickly that her grandfather had painted these fans
and did not give them to everyone.

Celia opened hers and admired the branch of plum blossom that had been painted across it. Sumiko's fan carried
a wisteria spray.

"Thank him for me," Celia said. "Tell him I think it's
beautiful and I will keep it always."

Sumiko translated and Mr. Sato nodded pleasantly. In
a moment Hiro's mother was back with a tray on which
were set a flowered teapot, small cups without handles,
and a plate of the prettiest cakes Celia had ever seen.
They were pink, green, white, and pale tan, each one
shaped in the form of a four-petaled flower. The girls were
supplied with cups of green tea and offered the cakes.
Celia chose a green one and saw that it was made of two
pieces of fragile crust as light as puffed wheat, with a
green jam in between.

The cake was almost too pretty to eat, but Sumiko had

bitten into her pink one, so Celia followed her example. It was crunchy and went to nothing in her mouth, but she liked the sweet paste in the middle.

"The cake is made of soy flour," Sumiko explained, "and the inside is a sort of jam made from soybeans. They call this sort of cake *monako*. Good, isn't it?"

Mr. Sato fanned himself with the somewhat larger-sized fan that gentlemen used, and beamed at them. Then he spoke to Sumiko in Japanese.

"He says you show talent in your drawing," Sumiko said. "My grandfather wants to know if you are planning to become an artist."

"I—I don't really know," Celia faltered. "I love to draw and I'd like to do something with it when I grow up if I can. But it's too early to tell."

There was a lengthy translation into Japanese. Then Mr. Sato spoke and again Sumiko translated for Celia.

"Grandfather says it isn't too early to tell—that you have natural talent. If you want to work hard and give your life to it, you can become an artist."

Not being sure what she wanted to give her life to, Celia was silent, and Mr. Sato spoke again. This time Sumiko looked at her curiously as she repeated his words in English.

"It's a funny thing, but he has hit on something I've felt about you. Only I never knew how to say it. I can see what he means in Japanese, but it's hard to change it into English. He thinks you are — well — tuned to the people and the world around you."

"Tuned?" Celia repeated, puzzled.

"He means that you truly see what you look at. He thinks most people don't. He says you sense what people are like, back of their words, behind their faces. He says there was a thread of deep understanding and appreciation between you and him that day he met you near the shrine. This does not happen to him with very many people. Because you have it, you should try to paint pictures so that others will experience what you feel."

Celia grew pink with pleasure, though she wasn't altogether sure she understood what Gentaro Sato meant. Anyway, it was wonderful to know that this important and obviously noble person liked her.

Now Mr. Sato turned to the tier of drawers beside him and took from one of them an almost square piece of stiff cardboard. A hair-thin band of gilt paper bound the edges all the way around. One side of the board was smooth and sprinkled with silver speckles. The other side was a white surface made for painting.

"He's going to paint a picture for you," Sumiko whispered in a tone of excitement. "This is an honor."

Celia held her breath as the artist selected a brush, moistened it, and dipped it in water-color paint. He held the piece of cardboard at an angle against his knees as he knelt on the cushion and touched the brush to the white surface. Watching, Celia could see the purple blossom of an iris come to life in only a few strokes of his brush.

Gentaro Sato glanced at her rapt face and then nodded toward the tokonoma — the alcove of honor. A blue vase held a single iris flower and a few green leaves. Celia remembered and knew what he meant.

"Your teacher," she said softly.

He laughed with pleasure and made a gesture for her to watch. Carefully he dipped a fresh brush into green paint on one side, turned it and dipped a touch of yellow on the other side of the brush. Then he made a single swift stroke down the paper, from the sharp point of the leaf at the top, to the broad base at the bottom — and a marvelous thing had happened. The leaf began in dark green and then shaded off into yellow along one side, green on the other. He had shaded it and painted two colors into it, all in one stroke.

He performed the same thing with several other leaves and the stalk of the flower, then drew a few lines of black here and there and the picture was done. As lovely a painting of iris as Celia had ever seen.

Finally he took a brush and black ink and stroked in the characters of his name. From a small black box he took a tiny seal, pressed it into the red paste the box contained, and stamped a seal below his name.

" What's that? " Celia asked.

" It's the personal seal an artist uses," Sumiko said.

With a low bow he presented the painting to Celia.

This time Celia didn't bother about translations. She spoke directly to the artist and put her heart into her words.

" Thank you so very much! I'll put this up in my room when I go home and I'll be proud of it and remember you."

If he did not understand all the words, he understood what her eyes were saying and her tone, and his smile was warm and friendly. Again he spoke in Japanese, and this time Sumiko looked a little uncomfortable as she translated.

" He says he does not like all Americans. He says they are sometimes noisy and impolite and have no respect for his gods. But you have made him stop and think that perhaps he has judged without knowing very many. He thinks your grandmother must be a fine lady. He has heard about the book she is writing."

For just a moment Celia thought of mentioning the fact that Gran wanted to meet him, but decided quickly that this was not the time. Besides, Sumiko was continuing, sounding a little annoyed.

"He is glad that you are my friend. He thinks you may be good for me."

"I wish I could talk to him," Celia said regretfully. "I wish I could tell him what a good friend you are, Sumiko, and how much I like you."

Sumiko shrugged. "I can't tell him that. And he probably wouldn't believe you anyway."

The old man spoke again, gently, and as she listened Sumiko's expression softened.

"He says that the beauties of nature have grown more dear to him than ever, for they contrast with the suffering Japan has known. He hopes that one day all nations will live at peace with the beauty about them and not try to destroy it."

Celia nodded solemnly. He was a wonderful old man. Sumiko was lucky to be his granddaughter. But now, she knew, they ought to go. She had been here long enough.

Sumiko, however, stopped her. "Wait, Celia. You haven't shown him the dragons yet."

Remembering, Celia took the two little pictures from her pocket and held them out to the artist. Sumiko explained that Celia had found them in a box that came from the storeroom of the former Sato house. Did her grandfather know what they were?

Gentaro Sato took the tiny pictures and stared at them for a long time. Watching him intently, Celia saw no change in his expression, but she had the quick instinct that the sight of these drawings disturbed him greatly. When he looked up, his eyes were dark and stern, and she knew that she was right. He spoke in a low voice and Sumiko had to lean forward to catch his words.

"He says he drew these very pictures many years ago. He copied them from something real in his possession."

The old man seemed suddenly older, and though he hid his emotion, he looked so shaken that Celia wished she had not shown him the pictures.

"Perhaps he'd like to keep them?" she asked Sumiko.

He accepted the drawings and thanked her gravely, but when Celia started to rise from her knees, he stopped her and spoke quickly to Hiro's mother. For a moment Mrs. Sato looked so shocked that Celia thought she might refuse to do whatever he had asked. But old habit won out, for Gentaro Sato was head of this household. She rose smoothly from her knees and went to a cupboard at one end of the room. From it she brought a handsome stand of black lacquer and placed it near the artist. It was made in the form of a wide base, with a support rising at each end, making a rack. Next she reached into the cupboard again and brought out what looked like the long scabbard of a sword. It curved to fit a blade it had once held, and along its length several crests had been etched in gold. Glancing at Mr. Sato's kimono, Celia saw that the leaf design of the crest on the sword sheath was the same as that on his kimono sleeves.

Carrying the sheath reverently, Mrs. Sato knelt and placed it, empty, upon the lacquer stand.

Gentaro Sato picked up a brush of India ink and drew something on a piece of paper before him. Celia saw that it was a sword, sheathless, with the naked blade exposed.

Mrs. Sato murmured softly in a shocked voice. " Ma-a-a," she said. "Long time now he never draws sword. Only flowers and birds."

The artist paid no attention to her. With the handle of the brush he tapped the hilt of the pictured sword and spoke to Sumiko in Japanese.

"This is the sword of our family that he has drawn," Sumiko said softly. "These *menuk*i — the little dragons — were set in gold and silver upon the hilt. Once, long ago, he drew these pictures of them for his own pleasure, and his eldest son, Hiro's father, saved them. But the sword is gone. He told Hiro's father that it must never fall into enemy hands and be used against Japan." Sumiko paused in her translation for a remark of her own. "As if we'd fight with Japanese swords!" Then she went on. "Before Hiro's father left Kyoto, Grandfather ordered him to destroy the sword. Now he is worried about having given this order."

Suddenly Gentaro Sato startled them by rising to his feet and crossing the *tatami* to the veranda that faced out upon the alley. He moved the reed blinds aside and Celia saw that he could look directly down into the garden at the rear of the Bronson house. When he turned back to them his expression was sad, but his tone was gentle when he spoke to Sumiko.

"He thanks you for bringing these pictures to him," she said. "He would like to keep them. But he is concerned because he feels that the spirit of his ancestor has appeared several times in order to tell him something — and he doesn't know what the spirit wants. Now it hasn't come for some time and he is troubled for fear he has failed it in some way that he cannot tell."

Celia had an eerie feeling as she listened. She could almost see that figure in the garden again, the pale face, the hazy drifting movement, and the sudden way in which it had disappeared.

She stood up, not wanting to hear any more, and Sumiko rose with her. They bowed low to Mr. Sato before they left, and Celia thanked him again for his hospitality and for the painting. Sumiko came with her downstairs and waited while Celia put on her shoes.

"That was sort of spooky, wasn't it?" Sumiko said, her eyes wide and frightened.

Celia nodded. "We've got to find some way to stop Stephen from having that *o-bake* night he keeps talking about. I — I'm afraid of what might happen."

13. O-Bake Night

*W*HEN her shoes were on, Celia stood up on the wide steppingstone that was placed on the ground at every Japanese threshold. She was reluctant to leave Sumiko. There were still things she wanted to talk to her about.

"Do you have to go back inside?" she asked. "Could you come out for a few moments? There's something I want to show you."

Sumiko asked her mother and was permitted to accompany her friend. However, Celia did not lead the way across the alley to their house, but turned uphill.

"It's only a little way — something queer I found up here in the woods. I wonder if you've seen it."

By some chance Sumiko had never taken the left-hand path. As they walked behind the bamboo fences and up the hill, Celia thought about the crests she had seen on the scabbard.

"Did you notice that those white crests were the same?" she asked. "I mean on your grandfather's kimono and on the sheath for the sword?"

Sumiko nodded. "That is his family crest."

"The pattern keeps reminding me of something," Celia said.

Sumiko, however, was not thinking of crests. "My

grandfather has never given me a painting," she said in a low voice.

There was something almost wistful about her tone, and Celia glanced at her in surprise. " I shouldn't think you'd care, since you don't like things that are Japanese. He must feel that too and believe that you aren't interested."

Sumiko tucked her blouse in around the belt of her plaid skirt with an impatient gesture, the wistfulness gone. " That's right — I'm not! "

" You'd probably have to let him know you'd like one," Celia said, ignoring her friend's words and speaking to what lay behind them. " I think he's wonderful. Such a fine artist and so very kind and understanding."

" You don't have to live there as his granddaughter," Sumiko said shortly.

Celia let the matter go, for they had reached the small clearing in the woods where the angry stone man raised his sword and screamed soundlessly, the snarling dogs crouched at his feet.

" Look," Celia said softly. " This is what I wanted to show you."

Sumiko stared at the scene and shivered. " I sure wouldn't want to have that fellow mad at me. I wonder why he's tucked away in the woods like this? There's no gate to show that it's a shrine."

Above the stone man a tall ginkgo tree pointed toward the sky and, as they watched, a breeze stirred its leaves and set them twinkling. All about them the wood rustled in the wind, and here in this dark hollow it seemed suddenly chill and dank.

" I don't like it here," Sumiko said. " Let's go."

Celia was willing, but this time she did not run, remembering her previous fall. She looked about for the root that had tripped her and saw that here the grass had been trampled. Suddenly she bent to look more closely. There before a shaggy bush was the clear imprint of a bare foot set in the earth.

"Someone else has been up here," Celia said. She remembered Hiro and the way he had not wanted her to take this path. Had he, for some reason, not wanted her to see those queer stone figures in the woods? Did he come here alone, and was this footprint his?

But Sumiko was anxious to get away and thought nothing of the footprint, so they went back to the sunlight of the alley and Celia returned to the house.

In the living room Gran was talking to Stephen.

"I really don't suppose there's any harm in staying up for one night, if that's what you want to do. Though I must admit that it seems a bit futile to me. If this Japanese ghost had the reputation for appearing every night at a certain hour, then I'd even be willing to stay up and watch with you. But to pick out just any night and stay up to catch him doesn't seem very sensible."

So it was the *o-bake* night they were talking about, Celia thought. Stephen really meant to go through with it.

He rumpled his fair hair and looked through the window into the garden. "I know — but Hiro says it appears when the moon is right. When it shines into the garden late at night. If it isn't misty tonight this might be the time."

"Oh?" Gran's eyebrows went up. "Then Hiro has seen this apparition too?"

"Well — no. But everybody at his house knows when it has appeared because of the way his grandfather acts the next day — excited and keyed up. The others in the house haven't seen anything because you can only look into our garden from upstairs, where Mr. Sato's rooms are."

Gran smiled suddenly. " Who am I to interfere with scientific research? Bring Hiro over tonight if you like. I hope you'll be reasonably quiet and not keep Celia and me awake for the whole watch. Hello, Celia. How did your visit with Mr. Sato go? "

Celia wanted to put into words her uneasiness about the *o-bake* night, but she knew Stephen would only laugh at her. She wished it weren't happening as soon as tonight. Now there was no way to stop it.

She gave her grandmother an account of the morning and showed her the iris painting and the fan. Even her brother looked at those things with some respect and said he'd like to have seen the iris painted. The only thing she omitted in her telling was Mr. Sato's remark about her being " in tune with people," and what he had said about the spirit of his ancestor.

Gran listened to it all with interest. " You were perfectly right not to bring up the subject of my book this time. There'll be another opportunity. By the way — you and Stephen haven't been to Kiyomizu Temple yet, have you? That's one of the most beautiful sights in Kyoto. Why not make plans to go there next week? It's not so very far from here."

Stephen said, " Sure, I'd like to go." But he cast a wary look at his sister and Celia knew he was thinking that if he took her along she'd do something foolish so that he'd be sorry she was there.

She turned away, trying not to feel hurt and a little guilty. Was it always this way with brothers and sisters? she wondered. Sometimes she had the feeling that Stephen didn't really like her very much and that nothing she could do would ever please him. That thought made her ache a little because she truly loved and admired him, and wanted very much to win his approval.

During the afternoon it began to rain, and Celia found herself hoping there would be no moon so the *o-bake* plan would be called off. But before dinner the drizzle lessened and a wind began to blow the mists away. By dark the rain was over. There were stars out in the windy sky and the moon would be up later on.

Hiro came over during the evening, his expression anxious behind his glasses. He had explained to his grandfather that American boys oftened visited each other's houses overnight, and Mr. Sato had given his consent. But of course, Hiro explained, he had said nothing to his grandfather about the real purpose of the visit.

Before they went to bed, Stephen announced that he and Hiro were going to take a good look at the garden. When they went outside, Celia took off her socks and slipped into a pair of geta instead of her shoes. She had been wanting to see what it was like to walk around in these clogs, and they would keep her above the mud and wet grass.

At first it was hard to keep the cloth strips between her toes, and she felt as though she were trying to walk on stilts. Then Tani, who stood watching in the vestibule, laughed and came down to show her that she was supposed to tip forward on the clogs with every step. Only then could Celia keep her balance and hold them on. This gave her a sort of rocking-horse gait as she clattered across the steppingstones after the boys.

Everything was damp and drippy and the scent of pine spiced the air. The big moon was rising like a golden bubble in the dark blue sky, and a faint radiance silvered the garden. Stephen, however, did not mean to rely on moonlight. He had brought a flashlight so he could probe every shadow, examine every dark corner.

" Do you think somebody could climb over the fence to play a trick? " Celia asked.

" That's what I want to make sure about," Stephen said, running the beam of the light along the stretch of bamboo fence that rimmed the alley. " I suppose it's possible, though he'd have to do some steep scrambling."

Hiro shook his head. " Makes much noise," he said. " You will be hearing."

" Maybe that's what woke you up the other time, Celia," Stephen suggested. " Do you think you heard someone climbing the fence? "

But Celia had no memory of any sound, either before or after she had seen the figure in the garden. Besides, an intruder would have had to climb out again and they would surely have heard that.

The gate was high and could be locked with a bolt as well as a key. Stephen himself locked it and the bolt made quite a rattle as he shot it across. Next they went around the side of the house and into the big rear garden where the figure had been seen.

" It could be," Stephen went on, " that you just saw that bomb shelter shining in the moonlight and thought that was your ghost. You do get awfully excited about things, you know."

Celia shook her head firmly. " The bomb shelter didn't wear a helmet and samurai clothes, or have arrows sticking out of it." She tried to sound sure, but she still wasn't certain of the arrows. What if the branches of the pine tree behind the bomb shelter had only looked like arrows? What if she had imagined all the rest too? She was no longer sure of anything, but she didn't want to admit that to Stephen.

The flashlight picked out every section of the garden. It lighted the space under the pine tree, startled the goldfish in the pond, made the stone lantern take a white shape in the glare.

"Another ghost," Stephen said. "Maybe it was the lantern you saw." And Hiro laughed in appreciation.

Celia didn't answer, and the light's beam slid along the rear fence on the side of the hill. If someone really wanted to get in, this might make a good place. But here the fence had been built higher for that very reason, and it seemed unlikely that anyone could scale it without a ladder. Besides, an intruder would have to make quite a thud when he leaped from the top of the fence to the earth, and that was something they would surely hear tonight, when they were alert to every sound.

Or at least the boys would be alert, Celia supposed. What she wanted most was to put her head under the quilts and sleep right through until morning. When she had entertained her romantic notion of a gentle lady ghost drifting through the garden like wind-blown mist, she had been fond of the whole idea. But she did not want to see the tortured face of her memory again. It had been too weird and frightening. Too unnatural.

Satisfied at last, Stephen led the way back to the house and they said good night to Gran on the way upstairs.

The *futon* beds were laid out in the middle of each room as usual, and the ginger cat was curled up at the foot of Celia's bed. She stroked it and listened to its reassuring purrs. It was still purring when she got into her pajamas and crawled between the quilts.

Through the thin fusuma she could hear Stephen and Hiro laughing and jumping around, as if they were practicing judo holds. Once Gran stepped onto the veranda and said softly that no *o-bake* would ever be so foolish as to appear tonight, unless they at least pretended to go to sleep. After that everything grew quiet.

But Celia could not sleep. She lay restless and tense, wondering if anything would happen. Neko-chan, the cat, must have sensed her restlessness and been disturbed by it, for after a while it left the foot of her bed and wandered away, its claws clicking against the straw *tatami*.

Around midnight the quiet was broken by the mournful notes of the *soba* man's flute, as he went his rounds offering bowls of hot buckwheat noodle soup to any who might be up at that hour. Always, always, Celia thought, no matter how far away from Japan she might be, she would remember those few haunting notes piercing the lonely quiet of the night. The flute and the sound of geta — these she would remember and they would always mean Japan to her.

Perhaps she dozed for a while. She could not be sure. Then, quite suddenly, she was awake again and there was the same prickling that had run through her before, warning her that all was not well. Beyond the paper shoji she heard a faint sound that was like someone crawling very softly along the veranda. So Stephen and Hiro were awake and listening too.

For a moment she was seized by an impulse to bury her head beneath the covers and hear nothing more until morning. But she had an even stronger desire to see what was happening. Soundlessly, she slid back the quilts and crept across the matting to the veranda. There, still on her hands and knees, she could peer between the rails down into the garden, yet without being seen from below. A sidelong glance told her that Stephen and Hiro had done the same thing. They too crouched there, watching the scene below in the bright moonlight.

A cold finger seemed to touch the back of Celia's neck as she realized that once again something was there in the garden. She saw the white, twisted face before she saw the rest. Then the samurai emerged, once more in full regalia, and she could not be mistaken about what she saw. The figure did wear a helmet — the horns stood up plainly in the moonlight — and the loose full trousers of the historical costume could be seen quite clearly. Again — as she had thought before — there were the arrows, piercing the wounded body, their tufted ends standing away from it.

The figure supported itself for an instant with one arm against the trunk of the pine tree — just as the warrior in the old picture had done. Then it staggered a few steps across the garden, and seemed to turn about helplessly.

The "nightingale floor" of the veranda squeaked and Celia glanced at Stephen, to realize in alarm that he was on his knees and that only Hiro's hand upon his arm kept him from rising. Hiro tugged at him and pointed across the alley. Celia looked toward the Sato house and saw that Gentaro Sato stood upon his own veranda watching the garden of the Bronson house. Once more his vigil had been rewarded and he too had seen the apparition in the garden.

Mr. Sato called out suddenly in Japanese, speaking in a strong, clear voice. It seemed to Celia that the ghostly samurai turned briefly in his direction and then away. A moment later it had faded into the shadows and the moonlight showed only an empty garden.

But now a light had come on downstairs in the Sato house and Celia heard a woman's voice calling out anxiously to see what was the matter. The artist stood a moment longer, his head bowed. Then he turned and went into the house to reassure his daughter.

"Let me go!" Stephen whispered, wriggling out of

Hiro's clasp. "I'm going downstairs to have a look. If there's anything there, it's still there. Come along, Hiro."

As he went past her on the veranda, Celia thought Hiro looked badly frightened and not at all willing to go down there where the ghostly figure had appeared. Nevertheless, he followed Stephen and they both ran down in their bare feet and out into the garden. Gran slipped into a *yukata* and came to stand sleepily beside Celia.

"What's happening, honey? Who was that shouting?"

"It was Mr. Sato," Celia said and found that her voice trembled. "The — the thing came again, and Mr. Sato tried to talk to it."

Gran put an arm about her and they stood close together, watching the beam of Stephen's light as he flashed it about the garden, probing the shadows as the moonlight could not. But there was nothing there.

Downstairs the ginger cat mewed plaintively, and now they could hear Tani and Setsuko stirring too — and there were more lights coming on across the way in the Sato house. Everyone was awake this time. Stephen could be heard reassuring Tani and Setsuko, and a moment later he and Hiro came back upstairs.

"We couldn't find a thing," Stephen said, his tone puzzled. "But there sure was something there — a samurai, just as you said, Celia. You didn't dream it after all."

Celia looked at Hiro, who had left off his glasses when he'd crawled from bed. His eyes squinted a bit when Gran turned on the light in her room and he seemed more nervous than ever.

"What did your grandfather say when he called out?" Celia asked.

Hiro gulped. "He — he say, ' R-r-restless spirit — what do you wish?' "

"I saw it, but I don't believe in it," Stephen said. He sounded baffled and a little angry. "It couldn't have climbed the fence as fast as all that. And there was no place else to go, unless it came into the house. I don't think it's hiding in our living room, or out scaring Setsuko-san and Tani-san."

"Well!" said Gran. "Ghosts or no ghosts, we're all wide awake and I'm hungry. How about something to eat?"

Hiro felt his stomach uncertainly, not sure that he could eat, but Stephen said that was a wonderful idea. Celia was willing too, so they all trooped downstairs and turned on more lights.

Setsuko, who was ready to get up and fix anything they wanted, had to be persuaded back to bed, and Tani had to be assured that Gran was not helpless and could do things for herself. She did too. The kitchen clock said two in the morning when they all sat down to a meal of scrambled eggs and bacon, toast, marmalade, and hot milk. And the food all tasted much more wonderful, Celia thought, than it ever could in the daytime. Even Hiro got over his nervousness about the ghost and managed to eat heartily of this Western food.

By the time their stomachs were full, the figure in the garden had once more grown less real, less believable. Gran talked about the strange things the mind could do. She said there had been occasions when people who thought they were going to see something impossible, really did. Like a mirage that was somehow thrown by the mind. There were so many things on this earth that men still didn't understand.

"After all," she said, "my own grandmother would never have believed in radio, let alone television. For all we know, this is something like that. Perhaps it's the very emotion that Gentaro Sato feels about this thing that projects some sort of vision."

She got quite carried away with this notion, though secretly Celia felt she was making things up as she went along. After a while her voice began to make everybody sleepy and they decided to go back to bed. Whereupon Tani, of all things, got up and washed the dishes!

This time Celia fell asleep with a clear purpose in mind. And she was awake before the rest of the household in the morning, even though she had missed some sleep. She put on a cotton *yukata* and went down to the garden. Inch by inch she went over the ground that Stephen's flashlight had covered last night. And she found what she was looking for — prints of bare feet in the still-damp earth. But unfortunately they were all over the place and clearly belonged to Stephen and Hiro, who had come dashing out last night without bothering with shoes or geta. So nothing was to be told by that.

Then, just as she was about to give up and go back inside, the early morning light struck something that gleamed in the grass near the bamboo trees. She pounced upon it in triumph and picked it up. It was an arrow. A perfectly real and unghostly arrow. And she was pretty sure that the ghostly spirit of a samurai wouldn't go around stuck full of real-life arrows. There *had* been someone in the garden last night. Someone alive and dressed up to represent a samurai. How he had made his way in, and where he had gone, was the real mystery. Where could he have hidden? How could he have disappeared?

The only place she could think of was the bomb shelter. She ran over to the door and shook it vigorously. It was locked tightly as ever.

14. The Temple of Kiyomizu

CELIA did not show the arrow to anyone. She took it upstairs before the others were up and hid it in the darkest corner of her closet. If she showed the arrow to Stephen, she knew the whole mystery would be taken out of her hands. Now let him puzzle about the samurai, while she went ahead and solved the mystery herself. That would prove once and for all that she wasn't so dumb. Then he'd have to give her some credit.

If she could solve it.

During breakfast, however, she changed her mind about one part of her decision. That was because of Gran's attitude, which had reversed itself since last night. This morning Gran was in a practical mood and somewhat worried about what had happened.

"I don't like to call the Japanese police into this," she told Celia and Stephen. Hiro had gone home before breakfast. "There would be such a commotion. Japanese is a language of rather vague ideas, and everything has to be said several times in different ways to arrive at one meaning. Besides, the police might decide it was really a ghost and not do anything about it."

"It wasn't a ghost," Stephen said positively.

Celia agreed, but she kept still. After breakfast, when

145

Stephen had gone off for his judo lesson, she took the arrow into the living room and laid it beside her grandmother's typewriter.

"I found it in the garden," Celia said. "I went down early this morning and looked."

Gran turned the arrow about in her hands. "Good for you. This may help us out. You know what it is, don't you?"

"Why — it's an arrow. And that samurai thing had arrows sticking out of it."

Gran nodded thoughtfully. "That's true, but this arrow isn't much like the terrible weapons the real samurai used to fight with. It would only get by in the moonlight when no one could look at it too closely. This is the sort of arrow American children play Indian with. Let's ask Setsuko-san and Tani-san if they know anything about it."

So the arrow was shown in the kitchen, though Gran didn't explain where it had been found.

Tani recognized it at once, her plump face alight with smiles. "Belongs small boy last famiry staying here. Must be is getting lost."

Someone had found it and picked it up, Celia thought. Someone who wanted to play a prank. Perhaps the boy in the last family had left a whole quiver of toy arrows behind.

Gran led the way back to the living room. "If someone is playing a joke, it may be harmless enough," she said. "So let's not say anything for a few days and see what happens. It may be that between them the boys and Mr. Sato gave whoever it was a good scare last night. Our ghost may think twice about reappearing."

So it was left at that, and Celia put the arrow away again.

When Sumiko arrived on Mrs. Nomura's heels for the doll lesson that day, she brought the unhappy news that her grandfather was ill. Hiro had refused to tell Sumiko exactly what had happened during the *o-bake* night, but she gathered that her grandfather had seen the samurai figure and had tried to call to it. Now he was terribly upset because he didn't know what the spirit wanted. He had a fever and had gone to bed.

Mrs. Nomura, listening to Sumiko, nodded wisely. " If place of sword is not found," she said calmly, " Gentaro Sato getting very sick. Maybe dying."

" Don't say a thing like that! " Sumiko cried, and Celia saw that she was near to tears.

" Why you not going to fortuneteller priest and finding out where is sword? " Mrs. Nomura asked, holding up Celia's doll approvingly to admire the work she had put into her sewing.

" Fortunetellers! " Sumiko cried impatiently. " Because I'm American, that's why, and I don't believe in Japanese fortunetellers. Besides, if Grandfather ordered Hiro's father to destroy the sword, then there isn't any sword to look for."

Mrs. Nomura put the doll down gently and looked at Sumiko with calm, untroubled eyes in her finely wrinkled face.

" Is very hard to destroy sword," she said gently. " Maybe so spirit wishes to know place of burying."

Sumiko stared at the little woman tearfully for a moment. Then she dabbed at her eyes and said she was sorry. Mrs. Nomura accepted her apology quietly and went on to other matters.

Soon the summer festivals would begin in Kyoto, she said. There would be the great Bon Festival first — the

Festival of the Dead — when everyone paid respects to
his ancestors. There would be processions, dances at the
shrines and in the streets, and people would come from all
the world to see these marvelous sights. Celia and Sumiko
were fortunate to be in Kyoto at this time.

Mrs. Nomura made an imaginary festival procession for
them with the two dolls right there on the *tatami*, and
Celia knew that she was trying to distract Sumiko from her
worry about her grandfather.

The festivals would include the night of bonfires — the
night of Daimonji in particular. They would see a great
and famous sight then.

Celia remembered the day when they had been on the
roof of the department store and the burned place had
been pointed out on the hill. All this sounded exciting and
colorful. She hoped Mr. Sato would be well again so that
he could enjoy these happenings.

When Mrs. Nomura left, Celia gave Sumiko the details
of what had happened the night before. But she did not
show Sumiko the arrow. If word of it got to Gentaro Sato,
it might make him worse, instead of better. She had a
strong feeling that even though it upset him, he needed to
believe in the samurai spirit. If he knew it was only a joke,
the knowledge might disturb him all the more.

In the next few days Gran too began to talk about the
coming excitement of the festivals and dances. Kyoto
would explode into color, and they would see such magnifi-
cence as they had never imagined possible.

"Let's get in our visit to Kiyomizu before the throngs
arrive," she said. "Perhaps Hiro and Sumiko would like to
come with us. I'm going to talk with a Buddhist priest up
there, so we can all go together. Then you young people
may wander around by yourselves and meet me later. And
of course you must each get a *stampu* book. You can get

them on the little street of stores going up the hill."

What a *stampu* book was, Celia didn't know, but Gran turned to other matters just then and Celia forgot about it until the day when they were climbing the hill to the beautiful Temple of Kiyomizu — the Temple of Clear Water. It was another uncertain, rainy-season day. There had been grayness and mists earlier, then patches of sunshine. But no one here ever seemed to stay home because of threatening weather.

Sumiko, much to Celia's disappointment, didn't come after all. She was worried about her grandfather, and Hiro said sadly that the old man was no better. As Celia was beginning to discover, the supposedly unemotional Japanese was a very emotional person indeed. He might hide emotion, lest it disturb and offend others, but his feelings were quite often very near the surface.

The steep hill that led to the temple was lined on both sides with tiny, open-front shops. There were shops selling ceramic masks, teacups, dishes of all sorts. This was Teapot Hill, the main pottery street of Kyoto.

In a shop near the top of the hill they stopped so Celia and Stephen could buy *stampu* books. The book Celia chose was a small one, about three and a half by four and a half inches. It was bound attractively in blue patterned silk. There was no spine to the book, since it opened on both sides and the pages could be pulled out accordion fashion till they were all exposed. Stephen's was green and a little larger. The shopwoman had an assortment of various-colored stamp pads and an array of stamps, and she proceeded to stamp page after page with the seals of various places they had visited around Kyoto. There was a little blue picture of Nijo Castle, a square mulberry stamp of Yasaka Shrine, and so on.

"The Japanese have a lot of fun with these books,"

Gran said. "When they go on a trip they dash out of a train the minute it stops in a station and get the station man to stamp their books. For a gift of a few coins you can have them stamped at any temple. It was the temples that started the idea."

Now the street ended at the foot of wide steps and high above rose the buildings of the temple. A tall red pagoda towered directly over them. To their left was a small building with several little images sitting outside, and as they watched, Celia saw a man come up to pray. The head of one of the small gods was turned the wrong way, so the suppliant took it in his hands and turned it about so that it was watching him. Then he clapped his hands and said a prayer over them, now sure of the god's attention.

Stephen started to laugh, and Gran hushed him quickly. "Don't forget that the things we do seem every bit as funny to the Japanese, but they are at least polite enough not to laugh in our faces."

Up the steps they went, along with streams of Japanese tours constantly pouring into the temple ground. Like Stephen, most of the men in the crowds had cameras, and frequent pauses were made so that everyone could take pictures. Beyond the red pagoda at the top was a fountain where a coiled bronze dragon spouted water, and here the devout stopped to rinse their hands and mouths before they went on to the temple buildings. Hiro was a Buddhist and he paused to do as the others did so that he could enter the temple grounds with clean hands and mouth.

At a gateway they paid a few coins and were given tickets in receipt — narrow strips of paper with a beautiful sketch of Kiyomizu printed upon them in delicate pink. It was like an equally beautiful green ticket that Stephen had brought home from Nijo Castle.

"Well, here we are," Gran said. "I'm going to have a look at the view and then I'll go to my appointment."

In front the temple had been built on an embankment held in by a great slanting stone wall, several stories high. But toward the rear it was supported by huge pilings made of the trunks of whole cedar trees, perhaps hundreds of them, towering into the air to hold the temple building on a broad platform.

Celia leaned beside Gran on the railing at the edge of the platform and looked out upon the tremendous view. Straight below was a deep ravine with a clear stream running through it and trees so thick you could scarcely see through them. Among the trees across the ravine rose a little pagoda. Beyond, to the right, lay the gray checkerboard of Kyoto.

The air was so clear and piny to breathe that Celia drew breath after deep breath, until Gran laughed a little.

"You'll be blowing yourself up like a balloon if you take in so much air. But I know how you feel. It's heavenly. And I see Stephen's having fun too, with his camera. It looks as though Hiro and you will have to stick together. Anyway, I'll meet you all in about half an hour — let's say the pavilion of Lafcadio Hearn's dragon. Hiro will know."

And off she went, hurrying to her appointment with the Buddhist priest in one of the many temple buildings.

Stephen wanted to take pictures and wander around to suit himself, while Hiro wished to say a prayer for his grandfather at a certain temple back under the hill, where there was a waterfall. It was a temple devoted to Fudo-myo, he said, and Celia, her attention caught because Fudo was the flaming god of her scrap of temple paper, went with him.

But this Fudo-myo did not look anything like the picture she had found in the lacquer box. This image too carried a sword, however, like both the picture and the little stone man in the woods. A notion seized her, and she felt in her pocket for the pencil she usually carried, but this time she had no sketchbook along. However, the *stampu* book would do nicely.

She opened it to one of the small white pages and drew a picture of the angry stone man, the crude stone lantern, and the two snarling little stone dogs, just as she had seen them in the woods. When she finished, she showed Hiro the picture.

"Do you know what this is?" she asked.

There was no change in Hiro's smiling expression, but behind his glasses his eyes blinked twice, rapidly. He didn't answer, pretending not to understand her question.

But Celia wouldn't let him off. "You know where these things are, don't you?" she persisted. "They're the figures in the woods back of our house."

Hiro continued to smile at her vaguely and Celia felt as though a door had been politely closed in her face.

"Is this a god?" Celia tapped the figure she had drawn.

This time Hiro nodded and gestured toward the waterfall behind him. "Is same god as here. Fudo-myo."

"The same one?" Celia repeated, puzzled. "But he doesn't look anything like this one."

"Artists make many pictures," Hiro said. "Same god."

"But why are those figures there in the woods where nobody goes?"

"To — to please the god," Hiro said haltingly. "Sometimes man builds small shrine for pleasing god. This one my family builds long time ago."

"Oh?" said Celia. "Is that why you didn't want me to go up that path the other day? Because it's a sort of private place and you didn't want me there? "

Hiro said a little stiffly, " I am not wanting you there."

Celia closed the *stampu* book, but she was not altogether satisfied. She had a feeling that she had put an answer into Hiro's mind and he had accepted it. But she still did not know the real reason why he had not wanted her there in the woods.

As if to change the subject, he picked up a light-green leaf from the ground and held it out to her. " You know what is this leaf? "

She recognized it at once. " It's from a ginkgo tree. Sumiko showed me one awhile ago."

Hiro nodded. " Is ginkgo leaf. But also is something else. Crest of Sato family. Like so." He found another leaf and placed them stem to stem to make a symmetrical pattern.

The family crest? Of course! That was why the crests at Mr. Sato's had reminded her of something. This was the pattern she had seen on the sword sheath, and also in the crest on his kimono. Both were stylized ginkgo leaves. And there had been a ginkgo leaf with the other things in the lacquer box. Excitement ran through her.

Suddenly, right out of the blue, she had the answer to something. The cardboard key — the ginkgo leaf. Now she had a clue that made everything fit together. Now she knew where the key to the bomb shelter was hidden.

15. Hiro

ℱOR a few moments Celia wanted to forget about Kiyomizu, Gran, Stephen, Hiro — and rush home as fast as she could go. But she would have to hide her impatience for now. There would be plenty of time for her search later.

As she and Hiro started back toward the main temple buildings, she tried to draw her companion out a little more.

"How is your grandfather today?" she asked as an opening question.

Hiro shook his head sadly. "I am saying prayer to Fudo-myo to give him strength in suffering," he said.

"You mean because of that samurai ghost and the sword?"

Hiro sucked in his breath. "Yes," he said at length. "If we can be finding sword it will be fine thing for my grandfather."

"But why? Why does the sword mean so much? He ordered it destroyed, didn't he?"

"I have poor Engris," Hiro said. "I cannot esprain."

He had lost control of several letters, but he went on anyway trying to "esprain."

"Buddhist rerigion — religion," he said, "is kind. Peaceful. Not hating. But Japanese also have Shinto. Many kind of Shinto. Before the war, miltary government is making all people believe in State Shinto. State Shinto is wanting war. My father does not rike — like. My grandfather does not like. But war comes. For country and emperor, my father goes to fight. My grandfather is sad and is no more making pictures of swords and samurai fighting."

He took off his glasses and began polishing them nervously with his handkerchief.

"But if your grandfather feels like that, then why does he want to find out what happened to the sword?" Celia asked. "I still don't understand."

"Sword is honor for famiry," Hiro said, putting on his glasses again. "Is no more for fighting."

None of this was very clear from the American point of view. But as Celia was learning, you couldn't understand other people just from your own point of view. You had to make an attempt to get theirs.

Anyway, the important thing seemed to be that Gentaro Sato was ill because he felt that his ancestor, the samurai, had come for the sword — which had probably been destroyed. But who was impersonating the samurai? Who could be playing such an unkind trick?

"Do you know who comes to the garden?" she asked suddenly. "I mean — who would dress up like a samurai to fool your grandfather?"

Hiro looked as downright shocked as though she had taken complete leave of her senses. He shook his head again and said nothing at all. So he too, like his grandfather, believed that the thing was really a spirit, rather than human. And how could you argue with someone who believed in spirits as easily as in reality?

Another Japanese tour streamed past them just then,

geta clattering over stones and earth. But Hiro was not watching the tour. His eyes had a faraway look.

" Last year," he said, " my grandfather takes me on train to Hiroshima."

Hiroshima? That was where the first terrible atomic bomb had fallen. Celia waited uneasily, and Hiro went on, struggling with his English, but managing somehow in the very earnestness of his manner to tell the story he wanted to tell. And as he spoke Celia forgot the worn thatch of Kiyomizu's steeply pitched roofs, the courtyards, and the thickly wooded hills. In her imagination she could see another scene that Hiro was building with his earnest words.

He made her see that now in Hiroshima there stretched a great empty plain of earth where the bomb had fallen. In the center of the plain rose a modern museum where hundreds of relics and photographs of what had happened were collected.

" In museum," Hiro said, " there is bamboo with gray shadow of leaves upon the stalk. But no leaves to throw shadows."

Celia shivered. She knew he meant that the shadows had been imprinted on those bamboo stalks by the action of the blast.

He went on and she could imagine solemn visitors moving through the museum, where no one laughed, or smiled, or talked very loud. There were Americans there too, elbow to elbow with the Japanese.

" But no more enemy," Hiro said. " Only war is enemy. Enemy of all people."

He told her then about the most moving moment of all — when he and his grandfather had left the museum and walked across the empty dirt plain to the place where the

Peace Monument stood. Here rose a canopy of concrete in modern design, sheltering the bronze casket beneath it. In the casket, Hiro said, were thousands of slips of paper bearing the names of all those who died when the bomb fell.

One after another, Japanese came to the railing before the tomb, placed sticks of incense reverently in containers of sand, to burn in honor of the dead, and then knelt to pray. Far in the background rose the domed skeleton of one shattered building which had been left standing as a reminder of what the rest had been after the bomb had fallen. All this in the heart of a new, modern city, abustle with traffic, its citizens busy and happy. And, strangely enough, with no resentment left against those who had dropped the bomb.

Hiro translated the characters on the casket softly into English and his pronunciation did not falter:

" 'Sleep undisturbed, for we shall not repeat this error.' "

There were tears in Celia's eyes. It was as if she herself had been to Hiroshima and stood before that tomb, weeping as many who came there wept, American as well as Japanese.

" Japanese believe those dying in violence do not sleep well," Hiro said. " But in Hiroshima we tell them to sleep, for this shall never happen again." He looked at her earnestly, almost pleadingly. " Japan makes error. America makes error. But these words do not mean to apologize for wrong. By ' we ' monument means mankind. It is *man* who must never make error again. You understand, Ceria-san? Is not for fighting my grandfather wants sword."

" I understand," she said gently. Gentaro Sato could not ever again think of a sword for fighting. More than any people on earth the Japanese had reason to hate and fear war. They wanted the people of other nations to hate it too and share their longing for peace.

She and Hiro were silent as they went back to look for Stephen.

Her brother saw them before they saw him, and he came toward them excited and triumphant. " You missed all the fun! You should have seen the fat fellow in a kimono who went through here a few minutes ago. I could tell by the way his hair was pulled back in that funny topknot they wear that he was a *sumo* wrestler. He must be very famous in Japan, because the kids were running up to get his autograph, and grownups were snapping pictures of him."

Stephen gave them a comical imitation of how the enormous fellow had looked, striding along, glancing to neither left nor right, very important, with his huge stomach stuck 'way out. Even Hiro recognized the impersonation and laughed out loud, his sober mood thrust aside for the moment. Celia was glad to have Stephen do all the talking. It gave her a little more time to return from the solemnity of Hiroshima.

" I got a picture of him right beside the dragon fountain," Stephen said. He glanced at his wrist watch. " It's time to meet Gran now. Where is this other dragon she was talking about?"

Hiro knew the place Gran meant. As they walked toward a stone torii and mounted a flight of stone steps, he told them the story that Lafcadio Hearn, the famous writer who had become a Japanese citizen in his later life, had written about this dragon long ago. Hearn had told how it could be heard weeping every night, and how in the morning the floor beneath was always wet with tears.

Two stone temple dogs stood at the head of the steps

and they went between them toward a small open pavilion. It was no more than a roof with a square expanse of floor beneath. Celia stood where she could peer upward at the ceiling and see the faint white markings that were all that remained of a very old dragon painting. The dragon coiled in a circle around the ceiling, but it was not crying now, and since it was not morning there was no dampness on the floor — only some smudged markings in the dust. Left there, perhaps, by the dragon's tears, Celia thought whimsically.

It was here Gran found them, very pleased over her interview. She had, she said, sat on the *tatami* in the priest's living quarters, while other members of his household watched television in the next room. He had been very gracious and had answered all her question and asked some of his own.

"So how do you like Kiyomizu?" Gran said. "You'll have to come back again and stay for a longer while. But at least you've had a glimpse of it ahead of the crowds that will arrive for the festivals next week."

On the way out, they stopped to have a priest mark their *stampu* books with a Kiyomizu seal — a tiny picture in maroon of the pagoda and temples. The sun came out briefly, low in the sky, shining on the peaked roofs, turning stone lanterns to gold, touching the fountain dragon's gleaming scales.

"There's no place like Kyoto," Gran said, drawing them to a stop on the steps going down, where they could see the whole city spread before them. "Aren't you proud to live here, Hiro?"

Hiro nodded and then glanced at Gran almost shyly. "Is better in United States? in New York? in San Francisco?"

"Not better," Gran said, "— only different."

"I wish to be going to America," Hiro said firmly. "I wish to be learning the good Engris and going to America."

Celia looked at him curiously. Behind his glasses his eyes were bright with eagerness and longing.

"But you wouldn't leave Japan for good the way Sumiko's father did, would you?" she asked.

"I will not be leaving for good," he answered promptly. "Japan today is becoming fine modern country. But I am wishing to see best things in America. Then I am bringing home new ideas for Japan."

"That's a fine plan," Gran said. "Perhaps if you make your grandfather understand what you want to do, he will help you to go."

"If you come to the States," Stephen said, "you'll have to visit us in Berkeley."

Hiro looked overjoyed and Celia had an idea that this earnest schoolboy would eventually manage what he hoped to do.

She was glad, however, when they left the temple steps and started down the street of little shops. Now all she wanted was to get home and find Sumiko. She did not want to search for the key alone. Sumiko must come with her.

16. Search for the Key

WHEN they got home Hiro went inside to see if Sumiko could come over to Celia's right after dinner. He brought back word that it would be all right, and Celia sighed with relief. She couldn't stand to wait until tomorrow, when the answer to so many things might be right at hand. Things she wanted to share with Sumiko.

Then, while she was eating dinner, the rain, which had threatened on and off all day, came down heavily and looked as though it would be an all-night affair. Celia groaned at the sound and Gran looked at her questioningly.

"Plans spoiled?" she asked.

Celia nodded. "Sumiko and I were going for — for a walk after dinner. Now we can't."

"What's so important about a walk?" Stephen asked. "You can walk any old time. Why don't you stay inside tonight?"

Celia shook her head, miserable with disappointment, and Gran looked sympathetic.

"Go for your walk anyway," she said. "If it's so important, you can put on raincoats, wear geta on your bare feet to keep you out of the mud, and carry Japanese umbrellas. I think there are some old ones around the house.

After all, you haven't had a real taste of Japan until you've gone for a walk in the rain under a Japanese umbrella."

The light came back into Celia's face and she smiled at her grandmother.

After dinner Stephen went off to his own room to work on his package of "Sorid Moders" with which he was building a battleship. "Sorid Moders" was really what it said on the box, but the term was plainly an adaptation of "solid models." At least he was busy and out of the way. He wouldn't be walking around in the rain himself.

Sumiko dashed across the street wearing her green American slicker, and she was willing enough to go for the planned walk. Tani, who would never have carried an old-fashioned umbrella herself, found two discarded ones for them to use. At the entryway the girls stepped into rain geta, which had wooden strips on the bottoms a bit higher than other clogs.

The umbrellas were made of strong oiled paper, stretched over a multitude of bamboo ribs. They were bigger than American umbrellas, giving the bearer a good circumference of dry area underneath. As the girls stepped into the downpour, the rain on the tightly stretched membrane of paper sounded to Celia like the beating of drums.

She did not explain what she meant to do until they were climbing the already muddy alley toward the woods. Then she had to shout above the roaring and spattering of rain on umbrellas to make Sumiko hear.

"Remember the picture of Fudo-myo?" she shouted. "And the other things in the lacquer box? The cardboard key and the ginkgo leaf?"

Sumiko, keeping her distance because of the width of the umbrellas, nodded vigorously.

"Hiro says the ginkgo leaf is the crest of your family.

So don't you see? The little stone man is also Fudo, and if I'm right — " But they had reached the edge of the woods, where the path began, and now they had to go single file.

It would get dark early tonight because of the rain, and the woods were already gloomier than she had expected. Always before she had seen them in bright daylight, or with sunshine slanting through the leaves. Now the trees looked forbiddingly dense and dark, the wet trunks gleaming like black ebony. Not for anything would she have come here alone at this time, but Sumiko did not seem worried by the fading light, or by the mysterious way in which the woods seemed to close about them as they took the left-hand branch that led to the little clearing.

It was only a short distance, but this path was overgrown with weeds that twined wetly about their feet and left green stains on their bare ankles. It was a good thing they were wearing geta which could walk over anything.

The stone man loomed at them with breathless suddenness. At one moment the trees and brush hid him, and then there he was beside the path, almost as if he had leaped from behind a tree, to stand there screaming at them in the rain. The cap of moss that covered his head was a wet, bright green and raindrops were splintering on the tip of his pointed sword. But if he really screamed at them now, they'd never hear it, Celia thought, what with all this uproar on their umbrellas.

She tilted her umbrella back so she could look up, and then called to Sumiko. "I knew there was a ginkgo tree here. That's what gave me the idea. I think the things in the lacquer box were meant to point the way to something. Only nobody recognized the fact and they've just been left there unnoticed all these years."

The ginkgo tree stood high above them, tall and dripping, pointing its branches to the sky behind the stone image. Gingerly Celia went up the crumbling steps and walked between the snarling little dogs. She had to stifle the uneasy feeling that they might snap at her with their ugly fangs. But Sumiko was there, and plainly Sumiko was not afraid.

"Maybe you're right," Sumiko said. "But what are you going to do?"

From the pocket of her slicker, Celia drew the garden trowel she had picked up before she left the house. "We're going to dig at the foot of the ginkgo tree. If you'll hold my umbrella over me, I'll start digging."

Sumiko looked astonished but interested, and she offered no objection. She held an umbrella in each hand, and beneath this double shelter Celia squatted at the foot of the tree and thrust her trowel into the ground. The earth was damp and soft, muddy on the surface, and gave way easily as she dug. But the task seemed suddenly much less simple than she had imagined. If her notion was right in the first place — and the combination of Fudo picture, cardboard key, and ginkgo leaf indicated this as the spot where the real key might be hidden — she still could not know the exact place in which to dig. How deep might the key be buried? In fact, how could she know exactly what she was digging for, since the key might well have been placed in some container first?

"Rest awhile and let me try," Sumiko said after a time. At least she wasn't impatient, or skeptical. She didn't say, as Stephen might have, that all this was nonsense — another crazy dream.

Celia changed places with Sumiko, but now, in spite of the umbrellas, they were getting wet and rather muddy, and every minute the woods were growing darker, until in a short while there would be no light at all. Celia suspected that Gran, in her generous suggestion about a walk in the rain, had not pictured exactly what they would be doing. But just as she was about to give up and tell Sumiko that they'd better go home, the other girl struck something with the point of the trowel.

She dug earnestly now and Celia bent above her, trying to make out what made that metallic ring when the trowel struck it. The last rays of gray daylight touched something in the hole with an unexpected gleam of golden light.

" What is it? What is it? " Celia cried, beside herself now with excitement.

Sumiko looked up at her and smiled. " Here — I'll take the umbrella again. It was your idea — you ought to dig it out."

So again they traded places, though this time Celia didn't care whether she was out of the wet or not. She could feel cool drops from the umbrella spokes dripping down her neck and she couldn't have cared less. For now the trowel was thrusting back the muddy earth to reveal the shape of a small bright box in the hole. Even with grime clinging to its sides, and green stuff all over it, the metal shone through.

" It's brass, I think! " Sumiko cried. " A little brass box! "

Celia reached into the hole and pulled it out. It was only a few inches long and not quite so many wide. Her fingers could feel the engraving on the lid, but now it was too dark to see anything here beneath the trees. With one wooden geta Celia stamped the earth back into the hole beneath the tree and they hurried away from the stone man, who was now a black shadow among other black shadows in the woods. She was almost fearful that he might reach out with his sword and pull them back, angry at this robbing of his treasure.

But nothing happened, and they clattered down the hill as fast as they could go and were soon out in the open again, where the daylight had not altogether vanished.

"Open it," Sumiko pleaded, taking Celia's umbrella again. "Let's see what you've got."

The lid stuck fast, but Celia managed to pry it up with the muddy edge of the trowel. Inside were several objects carefully wrapped in oiled paper. But this was no place to examine such small treasure.

"We'd better take this home to my room and look at it there," Celia said. "We'd better not unwrap whatever it is out here in the wet."

Sumiko agreed, and they clattered down the hill to the Bronson gate and hurried through. Lamplight in the house looked cheerful and welcoming as they reached the entryway. There the overhang of the roof sheltered them, and when they put the umbrellas down they felt practically deafened by the silence.

Tani came hurrying out to exclaim in dismay over their damp condition. She quickly brought a basin of water to sponge the mud and grass stains from their feet, and she hung out their wet slickers to dry.

As they passed the living room door, Gran looked up from the book she was reading, but she asked no questions. Celia kept the little box hidden under her arm until they were both in her room. Then they dropped down upon cushions to examine it. Beyond the fusuma Celia could hear Stephen, still working on his "sorid moder," and was glad that he was busy.

The little brass box had green scales of mould and verdigris embedded in the chrysanthemum pattern on its lid, but it didn't seem too much the worse for wear. Inside were the three little packages wrapped in oiled paper.

Celia chose one at random and unrolled the outer wrapping. There was still another inner wrapping of thin tissue and she unrolled that too, while she and Sumiko bent above the small thing in her hand.

In a moment it was revealed — a bit of gold and silver in the form of a tiny dragon, with its head turned as if it were looking backward. Swiftly Celia unwrapped a second package to show a second dragon, brother to the first, though individual in every detail.

"The *menuki*," she whispered softly, and Sumiko nodded and touched one of them respectfully with her finger.

"These must be from the samurai sword," Celia said.

Sumiko nodded. "The sword decorations were done by great artists in the making of swords. Each sword was different from any other. These are the same dragons as those in the drawings you found, aren't they? Celia — do you suppose whatever is left of the sword is buried up there too?"

"I don't know," Celia said.

She reached for the last small package and knew by the very shape and feel of it that this was what she had expected to find. She unrolled the strips of paper about it and revealed a tarnished metal key. In a moment she had brought the cardboard key from the lacquer box and compared the two.

This was plainly the original from which the pattern had been made.

"It's the key to the bomb shelter," Celia whispered. "I'm sure that's what it is."

"But why should anyone hide it up there?" Sumiko protested. " That doesn't make any sense."

" Maybe it does."

" But how? If anyone wanted to open the door to the shelter and didn't have a key, he could easily have the lock changed, or call in a locksmith to make a new key."

Celia balanced the key in her hand thoughtfully. " Maybe it wasn't hidden just to keep people away from the bomb shelter. What if it's only meant to point the way to something else? Something in the shelter? "

Sumiko was so still that not even her pony tail jiggled. She stared at Celia with her black eyes wide and attentive.

" Well — it won't take us long to find out," she said. " Let's go and try it."

Celia was sorely tempted, but after a moment's hesitation she shook her head. " It's still pouring rain. And this time there would be questions if we wanted to go — " She broke off because Stephen had come out of his room and was standing on the veranda watching them. Swiftly Celia closed her fingers over the key, glad that her hand was hidden from her brother.

" Hi, Sumiko," he said. " What did you two go out in the rain for? And what are you whispering about now? I could hear you through the fusuma — bzz-bzz-bzz."

Sumiko said nothing, and Celia giggled nervously. But Stephen had spied the *menuki* and he stepped onto the *tatami* and picked them up curiously. Clearly, however, they meant nothing to him, and after a minute he dropped them and went off downstairs, muttering that he was hungry.

Celia and Sumiko looked at each other for a moment and then laughed softly together. However, Stephen's interest in what they were up to stopped any further plans for the evening.

"I'll try the key tomorrow," Celia said. "I'll wait till no one is watching and then I'll open the door."

"You sound awfully sure," Sumiko said.

Celia smiled and said nothing. She was sure of the identity of this key clear through to her finger tips, but she didn't want to say anything more about it. The proof would have to wait until tomorrow. She had a feeling that she wouldn't want to explore a dank, dark bomb shelter at night anyway. It hadn't been opened for years and goodness knows what might be found down there.

She went downstairs with Sumiko and saw her to the door. Then she returned to her room, the key hidden tight in her hand. Morning was going to be a long time coming.

17. Festival of the Lanterns

THE GARDEN was fresh with the smell of earth and wet shrubbery after the rain. But the mists had fled and early morning sun made the bamboo shadows long and thin across the earth. Celia did not stop to dress, lest Stephen hear her and waken too, but came down in her pajamas and slipped into geta to cross the garden.

What she could see of the Sato house was as quiet as her own. No one appeared to be watching from the upper veranda. The key sagged heavily in the upper pocket of her pajamas. She pulled it out with fingers that were all too eager, and it slipped out of her hand and dropped into the mud. A moment was lost cleaning it off with the help of a few leaves. And then she was ready.

Bending before the low door of the shelter, she fitted the key into the lock. Because it was tarnished and a little rusty, it did not slip in easily, but she jiggled it this way and that and in a moment it was in place. Her guess had surely been right. This was the lock for which the key had been made.

It turned easily enough, though the squeak startled her. She put her hand on the knob and turned. Nothing at all happened. She pushed with the weight of her body, then tugged, but still the door resisted her.

It occurred to her that in the Orient things were often backward from the way they were at home. Perhaps it was the same with keys so that she had simply locked the door when she thought she was unlocking it.

Carefully she turned the key the other way and again there was a faint screeching of metal and the click of the bolt moving in the mechanism. This time she turned the knob with more confidence, but still the door did not budge.

Nothing she did helped in the least. This was certainly the right key and the right lock. The only contrary thing was that the door remained firmly locked. That didn't make sense — but it was clearly the case. Somehow or other the door was still locked.

She glanced up at the house and wondered for a moment if she should go and get Stephen. But Stephen would laugh at her for wanting to get inside an old bomb shelter. No — she would wait and consult Sumiko about this. Between them they ought to be able to think of some way to get the door open.

At breakfast time she ate in gulps, hardly able to conceal her impatience. But later, when she went over to the Sato gate to talk to Sumiko, her friend shook her head in a worried way.

"Grandfather is up," she whispered. "Though he really shouldn't be. This is the beginning of the Feast of the Dead, and he believes he is going to talk to the spirits of his ancestors. Hiro and the others, even my mother, are all behaving as if it were a perfectly everyday matter. Sh-sh — someone's calling me."

Sumiko ran back into the house and Celia went home in a troubled state, forgetting the locked door for the moment. What was the Feast of the Dead, she asked Gran, and why did Gentaro Sato think he must get up for it?

Gran pulled a plump red guidebook from the bookcase. " This will tell you all about the Bon Festival," she said. " The Japanese give it several names, but the one I like best is Festival of the Lanterns. It's a very beautiful and moving ceremony. Tonight we'll visit one of the cemeteries and see what's happening."

Celia took the guidebook outside and sat on a rock by the fish pond, reading. Once in a while she glanced in puzzlement at the shelter door, but since she could do nothing about it for now, she allowed her interest to be caught by the book.

For the coming three days, it seemed, the Japanese would invite the dead of every family to return to earth for a visit. They believed that the spirit world was never very far away, and that at this time the beloved dead could be led from the cemeteries where they slept and made comfortable and welcome in the homes they had left.

It was one thing, Celia thought, recalling Sumiko, to read about this and regard it as a quaint Japanese custom, but perhaps quite something else when a girl as American as Sumiko was expected to take a serious part in it. When she returned the book, she told Gran about how upset Sumiko had seemed.

Stephen heard them talking and offered his own comment. " Trouble with Sumiko is — she's neither fish nor fowl," he said.

Gran took off her blue-rimmed glasses and twirled them by their stems. " No, I don't think that's true. I believe her trouble is that she is *both* fish and fowl, and that's a pretty difficult sort of creature to be."

Twice that day, when she had a chance, Celia tried the key in the door of the bomb shelter, each time hoping she had somehow been mistaken. But it was no use — the door wouldn't open.

That night she and Stephen and Gran walked over to a cemetery on a nearby hillside, where many Japanese were gathering. The graves were set very close together and the whole place was prickly with the lettered name sticks thrust up behind every grave, giving the death names of those who were gone.

Tonight all the cemetery glowed with light, because every family had lighted white lanterns and hung them above the graves. Hundreds of sticks of incense had been lighted too, and clouds of smoke drifted in the glow of white light, the aromatic fragrance permeating all Kyoto.

Late in the evening the processions home began, for now the visiting spirits must be led courteously along the way, their path lighted by the many white lanterns, the rough places in the road pointed out, so they would not stumble. Everywhere sliding doors stood wide and small welcome fires were kindled before the houses as those who were loved came home.

It seemed to Celia that the people she saw taking part in the festival were happy and that everyone seemed kind and very considerate. But when she saw Sumiko, walking at the end of the Sato procession, looking rebellious and unbelieving, she knew that things were not going well with her friend.

Gran noticed Celia's concern. "When the three days are over," she said, "we'll invite Sumiko to dinner. I'd like to talk to her about several things."

After the festival Gentaro Sato did not return to his bed, but sat upon the veranda of his house, looking wan and thin as he stared into space for hours at a time.

By now the Satos seemed to take the friendship between Celia and Sumiko for granted, so when Sumiko was invited to dinner, no one objected. The nisei girl wore her best American nylon dress and the soft blue color was becoming.

"How nice you look, Sumiko," Gran told her. "But I'd like to see you in a kimono sometime."

"Thank you," Sumiko said, but made no comment about wearing a kimono. Celia knew she hated the idea.

Hiro had been invited too, and after dinner he and Stephen were going to another samurai movie down on Kawaramachi.

Setsuko made wonderful *sukiyaki* right on the table in Gran's electric frying pan, and they all ate with chopsticks.

Hiro was full of talk about more festivals to come. Early in August would come the night of Daimonji when the great bonfires would be built on the mountainsides.

"All will be beautiful," Hiro said. "Very fine for Americans to see."

Sumiko ate her beef and vegetables in silence and had little to say. Celia knew her friend was still troubled and wished she could help her. After dinner, when Hiro and Stephen had left, Gran slipped a hand through each girl's arm and drew them into the living room. They sat in comfortable rattan chairs, with the soft glow of Japanese lamps about the room, and now gently, without seeming to pry, Gran got Sumiko to talk about the things that were worrying her.

It seemed that the last three days had been especially distressing.

"Imagine!" Sumiko cried. "Grandfather really believes that the spirits of members of his family came home with us from the cemetery and lived in his house again. He talked to his son — Hiro's father — as though he were really there. And even to my father. Once I went upstairs and heard him in his studio. He was painting a picture, and talking to his sons at the same time. I don't like it! It's nothing but foolish superstition."

" Do you think *we* never talk to those who are gone? " Gran asked.

Sumiko stared at her in puzzled surprise.

Quickly Gran went on. " There's never a day passes that I don't remember my husband — Celia's grandfather. Sometimes I talk to him about my problems as though he were really here. And more than once I've had the strange feeling that he was advising me. There's something somewhere that understands my words, Sumiko. People aren't really so different, you know. It's only customs that seem strange to those who have other customs. If you'd been brought up in Japan, you'd accept these things just as Hiro does."

Sumiko clenched her fists together in her lap and Celia was startled by the sudden intensity in her friend's voice. Sumiko had never been trained to hide her emotions as Japanese girls were.

" But I wasn't brought up in Japan! " she cried. " I'm not Japanese and I never will be! "

Gran reached out and covered Sumiko's defiant hands with her own. It was a gentle, quieting gesture.

" That's where you're wrong," Gran said. " And I believe that you're old enough and smart enough to stop shadow-boxing and accept what is really true."

" Shadow-boxing? " Sumiko repeated blankly.

" That's right. Fighting shadows. Trying to make something true that isn't true. Trying to pretend that you're not Japanese as well as American."

" I didn't ask to be born the way I am," Sumiko said

almost sullenly, and now she would not look Gran in the eye. Celia twisted her handkerchief together uncomfortably, all her sympathy with Sumiko. She hadn't dreamed that Gran, who was usually so understanding, would talk to anyone like this.

"Not one of us asks to be born," Gran told Sumiko firmly. "Not one of us asks for what he regards as his special handicap. But every one of us has something he fights and thinks is wrong in himself. When I was a little girl I was the homeliest child in my grade in school, and I suffered over it terribly. Until I grew old enough to realize that I could make my own face with the way I thought and the way I acted."

Both girls looked at Gran in astonishment. She had so much life and eagerness and kindness in her face that Celia had somehow taken it for granted from the first that she was very attractive — as indeed she was.

Gran's eyes twinkled as she went on. "You can take Celia for another example," she said.

Celia stiffened and Sumiko threw her a quick look.

"Celia has everything," Sumiko said. "She's so pretty and fair-haired. She's *really* American, and — "

Gran broke in with affection for her granddaughter in her voice. "I agree. But our Celia has the curious notion that people think she isn't very smart and that the brother she looks up to doesn't care much about her. It's probably true that he doesn't care about her *consciously* right now. That's because he's busy with other things and takes her for granted. And he's at the teasing age that boys reach. But with another part of him that he isn't aware of himself, I'll wager he thinks his sister is just about the nicest girl ever."

Celia felt as if she were blushing clear to her toes. She

could even feel silly tears prickling back of her eyes. Because Gran knew. Gran had understood better than Celia herself had understood.

"You see," Gran went on, "Celia has to live with her handicap — that is, what she regards as hers for the moment — until in a year or so she'll find out it doesn't matter. Because the things we think are handicaps are only something to be lived with until they are overcome. We have to say to ourselves, as everyone else must: ' This is the way it is. I accept it and forget it. I'll go on from here and spend no more time moaning about what can't be helped unless I help it.' "

"But — but how can my handicap ever be overcome?" Sumiko wailed.

Gran put her arms on her knees and leaned forward earnestly. She held Sumiko's dark eyes steadily with her own gray ones.

"It will begin to be overcome the minute you truly accept the fact that you are *both* American and Japanese, and that because this is so you have something especially valuable to give to Japan. And maybe someday to give America too."

"You don't know!" Sumiko cried. "The Japanese don't like nisei. They think we're being superior. They think we think we're American and that we look down on them and — "

"And hasn't that been true? With you, I mean?" Gran asked.

Sumiko opened her mouth to answer and then paused. "Why — maybe it has. Only I didn't see it that way."

Gran laughed softly, the wrinkles about her eyes deepening. "Then you're not even being a good American, are you? Most Americans these days don't believe in prejudice, you know. We hate it and fight it in our own country and in ourselves. Sumiko, don't you see that you can't be a good anything until you're both a good American *and* a good Japanese? Of course that's a harder job than most of us have. But I think you're a smart enough girl to manage it."

" Both? " Sumiko echoed in a puzzled voice.

" Yes," Gran said. " I have several nisei friends here in Japan who are well accepted and well liked because they've earned the right to be. That's the only way any of us can ever expect to be liked — for what we really are."

Quite suddenly Sumiko put her head down in her hands and began to cry softly. " I miss my father so much," she choked. " I can't talk to my mother any more because she has gone completely Japanese. But I could always talk to him."

" You still can," Gran said. " You can talk to him just as your grandfather talked to him. And you can hear what he'd say to you in your own mind and heart. You know the things he might tell you, don't you — if you're honest with yourself? All you have to do is stop fighting yourself and listen. Perhaps this is something people out here have that we lack. They never forget those who have gone before. They go right on feeling close to them and making them part of their lives."

Sumiko wiped her tears away.

" You're young enough," Gran said, " to have plenty of time for thinking. I know you'll work this out. But now — let's go for a walk and catch the last bit of daylight."

As they went out, Celia remembered the key and the door that wouldn't open. But Sumiko was thoughtful and quiet, and Celia knew this wasn't the time to bring the subject up. Yet she could not be rid of her own feeling that

he door was still important. Important, somehow, to them
ll.

For the next few weeks festivals went on constantly, all
over Kyoto. The people seemed to enjoy this season so
much that they were reluctant to tie their activities to the
prescribed days of the celebration alone. Consequently the
festivities stretched on and overlapped at both ends of
the season.

One night Celia and Sumiko, Gran and Stephen attended an informal street dance that started up not far
from their house. Hiro was off on affairs of his own and so
not with them. Overhead bright stars shone in a windy
sky. Lanterns swayed, sending flickering light and shadow
over the gay scene. There were more kimonos out than
usual, and the girls looked like bright butterflies as they
followed the pattern of the dancing. That night there were
no "strangers." Hands were extended in welcome to take
them into the dancing circle. Laughter at mistakes was
good-natured, and steps were eagerly shown to these foreigners who wanted to take part in the Japanese festivities.
A victrola played Japanese songs over and over, and everyone joined hands in a sort of snake dance up and down the
street.

Rain had held off and tonight's high wind swept the
mists away and sent clouds scudding across the sky so that
lights sparkled with an intense brilliance, and there was a
tingle of excitement in the air.

It had been a day of running around for Celia and, since
Gran and Stephen wanted to stay longer, Celia and Sumiko
started home ahead of the others.

As they wound their way up the hill, they found their
own street nearly deserted, what with everyone being out
where the fun was going on. When they reached Celia's

house she was just about to bid Sumiko good night and
unlock the gate, when she heard a sound across the street
in the direction of the Sato house. Something prompted
her to draw Sumiko back into the shadow of the gateway.
The Sato house was dark except for a light burning upstairs in the artist's rooms. But as they watched, someone
darted out the gate and started up the hill in a great hurry.
It was Hiro, and he was moving so quickly and furtively
that the girls watched him in surprise.

He seemed to be holding something near his body, as
if to hide it from view. But as he turned the corner up near
the wooded hillside, Celia saw that the thing he carried
looked like a sword. But what in the world was Hiro doing
with a sword? And why was he behaving in so queer a
fashion?

"What's he up to?" Sumiko murmured. "And what's
that thing he's carrying?"

Celia shook her head, but she wondered if he could
have found the old sword his father had been told to
destroy. Was he perhaps taking it up to the little stone
god in the woods? Such action might well fit in with Japanese behavior.

"I don't think we'd better follow him," Sumiko said.
"But I'm sure going to ask him what he was doing when
he comes home."

They said good night then and Sumiko went across the
street. Celia unlocked her own gate just as a sudden gust
of wind tore along the hill and fairly blew her into the
yard. A light burned in Setsuko's quarters, but Celia didn't
go into the house at once. Instead, she walked around the
side to the windy garden behind and looked carefully
about in the reflection of light from the house. As far as
she knew, the samurai had not appeared since the night

when the two boys had watched for him. Probably they had given the masquerader a real scare and he had not dared to return. But still she liked to look when she had a chance, to make sure nothing else had been dropped as that arrow had been.

As she went past the bomb shelter she couldn't resist trying the doorknob, the way she usually did, even though she knew it was foolish. But this time the feeling of the knob in her hand surprised her. It actually felt as though the door might be open. At once she tried the knob again.

It turned easily in her hand and the door to the bomb shelter pulled wide open.

18. Down the Stairs

CELIA stood for a long moment, staring in astonishment at the steep flight of stairs leading down into the shelter. The gusty wind whipped her skirt against her legs and blew her light hair about her shoulders. It also blew the clouds away from the face of the moon and she could see clear down the stairs to the earthen walls and floor of the small chamber below.

Only the upper covering of the shelter appeared to be made of protective concrete. The stairs were of wood, and the room below had been carved from the firm red clay of the Kyoto earth.

Why did the door open now, when it had always seemed to be locked before? Had she been mistaken all along? And Sumiko too, when she had tried the key recently at Celia's request? Or could it be that their continued attempts had jiggled loose whatever had stuck, so that now at last it could be opened? Yes, that must surely be it.

Swiftly she glanced around. No one stood on the veranda of the Sato house. Setsuko was home, but out of sight, and Tani out at the dancing. In a little while Gran and Stephen would be coming back. Somehow Celia didn't feel a bit tired any more. She had to go down those stairs and see what was there in the bomb shelter. And she had to do it now, quickly. Then she would really have something to show Stephen when he got home. If she waited, she knew well enough what he would say: "Huh, so you were scared to go down!" And he'd brush right past her and make the secret place his own.

No, he won't, she told herself firmly. There wasn't a thing to be afraid of, with bright moonlight shining down the shaft. She would be the first one down and then he'd have to respect her courage.

Nevertheless, she stepped carefully onto the top step, testing it with her foot to make sure the wood had not rotted in all the years this place had been closed. But the step held firmly and didn't seem to be in the least rickety. One cautious step at a time, clinging with her hands to the steps themselves, since there was no rail, she started down. It seemed a very long way to the bottom. The air had the dank smell of earth about it, but with that wind blowing behind her the staleness had rushed out quickly, and the air wasn't stuffy and dead as she had expected it to be.

When she was only three steps down from the top, two startling things happened at the same time. The moon went abruptly behind a dark patch of cloud, so that the stairway and room below vanished from sight as if they had been suddenly erased. At the same instant something live and horrid and furry brushed against Celia's bare hand as it scurried past her on the stairs. She screamed wildly, reached for a stair rail that wasn't there, and went plunging into space.

The ground must have been ten steps down, and it was a long fall. The impact stunned her for a moment and she lay shivering with shock where she'd fallen, the earth hard-packed beneath her, pain streaking through her body. But she could not think of pain for the moment. She could think only of that live thing that had brushed against her skin. Had it been a rat — and were there others down there in the pitch-darkness? She must get out quickly. She mustn't cry or scream. She must find the stairs and get out!

But now, as she moved, the pain became more insistent and she knew that it came from her right ankle. When she tried to stand, pain stabbed sharply and she couldn't put her weight upon her foot. Nearby something mewed gently in the darkness, and she cried out in relief. The furry thing hadn't been anything unknown and horrible, after all. It had only been the ginger cat leaping past her down the stairs, ready to do some exploring of its own.

"Come here, Neko-chan," she called, laughing now in reaction and holding it tight as it came willingly to her. Its fur felt reassuringly soft and warm and it was wonderful not to be here alone in the darkness.

"I've got to get out," she told it. "Maybe if I try crawling on my knees . . ."

But the thin blade of pain streaked up her leg again and brought tears to her eyes. Had she broken her foot? Gran and Stephen would be home soon. Perhaps they'd come around this way to enter the house and she could call to them and let them know where she was. But even as she was thinking hopefully of their return, a heavy gust of wind whipped across the garden above, sending a puff of cool air down the stairs. To her horror the door slammed firmly shut.

What faint light had remained in the opening against the sky was gone and it was blacker than ever here in the shelter. She caught the cat to her in terror and hugged it until it mewed and wriggled out of her grasp. What was she to do now? With all that wind Setsuko wouldn't have heard her first scream, and now no one would hear her down under the earth. Gran would miss her as soon as she got home and worry. Perhaps she would go to the Satos', and then to the police, but neither she nor Stephen would ever think to look for her here.

Celia knew she had to crawl up the stairs somehow, had to escape from the black, frightening pit!

Painfully she managed to get onto her knees, but she felt so trembly and scared that the effort was doubly difficult. From this position on her knees she reached out hesitantly across the cool, earthen floor, afraid of what she might touch in the darkness. Something soft lay beneath her hand and she felt it gingerly.

There seemed to be a wad of cloth or clothing here. Perhaps in the days when they had expected to use this shelter, the Satos had put clothing or bedding down here in preparation. She pulled herself along on her knees another few inches and then waited, choking back her tears, until the throbbing pain subsided. Once more she reached out cautiously. She must be near the stairs now. If she could take hold of the steps they might help her to pull herself up to the place where she could open the door. How long would she be able to breathe down here in this hole, now that the door was closed? Though, strangely enough, it did not seem stuffy as yet. Perhaps the Satos had arranged for some means of ventilation.

Again she groped ahead with one hand, but instead of the stairs, she touched something that felt hard and stiff beneath her fingers — yet brittle too, as if it might crush if she leaned upon it. Her fingers felt over the strange contours — smooth hills and valleys — almost like the shape of a human face.

She felt the thing again. Yes, there were slits for eyes,

and humpy eyebrows above. There was a great beaked
nose, with slits for breathing. In spite of her hurt and
fright, excitement came to life in her. Before she touched
the mouth, she knew how it would be. She knew the tortured twist of those lips, the frenzy of suffering it would
reveal, and she knew what she had found.

This was the mask that the samurai had worn when he
came to "haunt" the garden! Now she swept a hand out
all about her, until she found the helmet. Everything was
here. This was the place in which he hid his costume for
his strange masquerade. So it was the "ghost" who held
the key to this strange place, and who had used the shelter in recent times. But who was he and why had he played
this trick on Gentaro Sato?

Suddenly startled, she became aware that a faint light
had begun to glow in the far wall of the shelter. *In* the
wall — not on it! She eased herself to a sitting position,
cold with new dread. Even as she stared, the light grew
brighter, sharper, and she knew that it came from the beam
of a flashlight. She did not scream again, although her
throat tightened with the effort to hold back sound.

She could see now that there was a small passage cut
through the hard clay earth — large enough for a man to
crawl through. Someone was creeping through it now,
pushing a lighted flashlight ahead of him. And who else
could it be but the samurai?

Something sharp and bright shone in the light, a pointed
tip of metal, emerging slowly from the tunnel. As she
watched in frozen fascination, the shining blade of a sword
emerged from the hole, until the thing was completely in
sight, with the hand that held it. A moment later the flashlight turned full upon her, blinding her, and she cried out,
shielding her eyes with her hand.

" Ceria-san! " cried an alarmed voice, and a moment later Hiro was kneeling beside her, looking down into her tear-stained face in dismay.

" Hiro! " she cried in relief.

" What is happening? " he asked. " How are you coming here? "

She explained breathlessly. " I fell off the stairs and hurt my foot. The door blew shut. And I thought you were the — the samurai ghost."

Hiro stood up and shot his beam toward the door above them. " Is not locked," he said in surprise.

She looked up and saw what he meant. Someone had put a hand bolt inside the door, and this must have been what held it when the key had seemed to work. All the time it had been locked from the inside.

" Must be I am forgetting to lock door," Hiro said. " And now you hurt foot, and all is for me to blame." He put a hand on each side of his head and rocked it back and forth as if it hurt him to think.

" Please call somebody," Celia begged. " Gran must be home by now."

He hesitated a moment. Then he put the sword he carried beneath the stairs, folded the mask and clothing together and wadded them out of sight beside the sword. Leaving the flashlight behind for Celia, he ran up the stairs. The cat came out of a corner and leaped out the door behind him, having had enough of bomb shelters.

This time the door stayed open and Celia could hear Hiro calling, could hear the welcome sound of Stephen's voice in answer. A moment later her brother scrambled down the stairs, to kneel on the ground beside her.

" Are you all right, kid? " he asked in a voice that broke unexpectedly. " You had us scared. We've been looking everywhere for you." He slipped his arms under her gently. "Will it hurt too much if I lift you?"

She shook her head. Now that he had come for her, the pain didn't matter so much.

"Hang on around my neck," Stephen said, "and we'll have you out in a jiffy. Don't be afraid. Everything's all right now."

She waited for him to scold her and tell her how dumb she was, but he only sounded kind and a little worried. Hiro put a sling of cloth around her foot and held it so it wouldn't dangle loose and hurt her.

When Stephen carried Celia into the house and laid her carefully on the couch in the living room, Gran took one look and hurried to the telephone to call a doctor. Sumiko was there too, because Stephen had gone across the alley earlier to look for his sister, and Sumiko had come back with him in alarm.

There was the usual "*moshi-moshi*" conversation over the phone, and the phrase "*chotto matte*" — "wait a minute" — was used several times. Then Gran got through to the doctor.

Now, for Celia, everything seemed to run along in a blur. Tani was home, Setsuko up. They made squealing sounds of dismay and ran about, getting in each other's way. Hiro apologized and apologized, though nobody but Celia really knew what he was apologizing for. The American doctor came and looked at her foot and said he thought it was only a sprain and nothing was broken. But it would have to be X-rayed and she must keep off it for a few days.

Between Stephen and the doctor they got her upstairs, and Gran tucked her under the covers of her *futon* bed. When the doctor had gone, Celia asked Gran urgently to send Hiro upstairs — not Sumiko, but Hiro. She wanted to talk to him, now that the pain wasn't so bad. She just had to talk to him alone.

If Gran had questions, she was wise as usual and saved them for later. She called Stephen downstairs and sent Hiro up. He came in and knelt on the *tatami* near where she lay and looked at her anxiously.

" I am so sorry," he began again and she hushed him quickly.

" It wasn't your fault, Hiro. But it was you in the garden dressed as a samurai, wasn't it? You were the ghost? "

He nodded sadly. "Prease you do not tell my grand-father."

" But why did you do it? "

Haltingly the story came out. It had all begun because Hiro had a belief that his father would not have destroyed the samurai sword, even though Gentaro Sato had ordered him to do so. To Hiro the famous sword was a family treas-ure and should be recovered. Stories of the past had always held his imagination, for all that modern Japan meant so much to him. He could not bear to think that this sword of his father's was gone forever. In his growing-up years he had always played the game of searching for it.

While the last American family had lived here, he had thought of a place where the sword might have been hid-den. In the mid-hours of the night he had climbed the bamboo fence into the garden of this house, while every-one was asleep, and he had tried to dig near the pine tree, of which his father had been very fond. But he had found no sword, and it was like looking for one grain in all the sand on a beach. The sword might be anywhere.

Only one person saw him that night. There was only the thin light of a small moon, but his grandfather had been wakeful and had made out a hazy figure in the garden. Gentaro Sato had taken the sudden notion that the figure that hovered near the pine tree was the spirit of his ancestor. Hiro said his grandfather had seemed happy the next day. His belief in the vision had seemed to do much for him. But now, to Hiro's dismay, he watched and waited for the next visit of the spirit. Of course Hiro couldn't risk climbing the fence repeatedly, but a plan began to evolve in his mind and he thought of another way.

He remembered the tunnel his father had dug from the bomb shelter to the hill back of the house. His father had felt that the shelter must have two exits. Then if the entrance were destroyed, those hiding in the earth could still crawl through the tunnel and escape into the woods on the hillside.

" The woods! " Celia cried. " Then the tunnel entrance must be up there near Fudo-myo, where I saw the print of the bare foot in the earth? "

Hiro nodded. " I am not wishing you to go there to find tunnel."

He went on to tell her how successful the masquerade had been. Through his uncle at the movie studio, Hiro had obtained a discarded samurai outfit and had hidden it in the bomb shelter. And he had bought a mask. The door at the top of the stairs was locked, but Hiro had managed to pick the lock and had fastened a bolt across inside, so no one would come down and discover his secret. Now he could appear briefly, be seen by his grandfather, and then disappear mysteriously into the black shadow of the shelter door, with no one being any the wiser.

But all had not gone well, and Hiro had done some secret suffering. What had seemed a simple way to make his grandfather happy began to take on difficult aspects.

Gentaro Sato worried because the samurai did not carry his sword. He began to feel that the "spirit" had some message for him and he became upset because he could not understand what was wanted of him.

"But you found the sword, didn't you?" Celia asked softly. "That was the sword I saw you carrying up the hill tonight — the one you brought into the shelter?"

"No," Hiro said, his tone sad again. "This sword is only play sword."

He had meant to hide it in the shelter and perform one more masquerade. He knew it was growing dangerous to appear, because the Bronsons were curious and Stephen might catch him at any time.

Celia remembered suddenly. "But, Hiro — you were with Stephen the last night the samurai appeared. The *o-bake* night. I don't understand —"

Hiro gave her twisted grin. "Is my frien' Michio," he said. "So you do not be suspecting, I ask Michio to play samurai. He is trusting friend. He does not tell. Seems very funny when we plan this. Not so funny later."

So that was it! "But what were you going to do with the play sword?"

Again he explained. One last time he would have dressed up and appeared. When his grandfather saw him, he meant to salute him with the sword and then disappear. He had hoped this would settle everything. His grandfather would feel that the samurai had recovered the sword of his fathers' and that all was now well. Then the spirit would be at rest and never appear again.

"And now this is no good," Hiro said. "Because I open door and forget to lock."

"And I fell down the stairs," Celia said. "But, Hiro, I think it would be best of all if you could find the real sword and give it to your grandfather."

He looked at her sharply. " *So desu*, this is best. But how I am to do this? You are knowing something? "

" I think so," she said. " I think you're right and your father didn't really destroy the sword. But if you don't mind, I'd like to tell Gran and Stephen and Sumiko about all these things too. It doesn't really matter if they know, does it? The secret has come nearly to an end."

Hiro bowed solemnly and agreed it did not matter. He did not think he would ever try the make-believe again.

So Gran and Stephen and Sumiko came upstairs, and when they were there, Celia asked Sumiko to get the two small boxes from the drawer in her dresser. The black lacquer box with the gold pine tree on its lid, and the little brass box corroded with verdigris. Quickly she told them the truth about the apparition in the garden, so Hiro wouldn't have to struggle with it again.

" That's all over now," she concluded, giving Stephen no time to break into questions. " But there's still one thing — the sword. I don't think it was destroyed and I think Mr. Sato ought to have it back. It might make him feel better. And I think I know where it may be hidden. All these things point the way."

19. Night of Daimonji

CELIA showed them the picture of Fudo-myo, who was also represented by the little stone man on the hill. And there were the ginkgo leaf and the drawings of the dragons, which Mr. Sato now had.

Stephen stared at her in surprised interest when she told how she and Sumiko had gone digging at the foot of the ginkgo tree one rainy evening. When Celia opened the little brass box, Hiro drew in his breath in surprise. Yes — those must be the *menuki* from the famous sword. They were works of great art. It was splendid to recover them.

"I kept thinking," Celia went on, "that if they were here with the key buried in this box, they must point to the bomb shelter. The *menuki* stand for the sword, the key stood for the bomb shelter."

"Do you suppose —" Stephen cried.

But Hiro was already on his feet and halfway out of the room. Stephen ran after him, but on the veranda he paused and looked back at his sister.

"Don't worry — if there's anything there, we'll bring it to you first. After all, you're the one who was smart enough to figure it out."

And off he went, leaving Celia blinking. Sumiko went to the veranda rail where she could watch the boys as they climbed down into the shelter. Gran, sitting on a cushion close to Celia, reached out and held her hand for a moment.

"Little did I know that I was going to have a Japanese mystery right in my own house. Are you comfortable, honey?"

Celia nodded, her eyes bright. The throbbing in her ankle hardly mattered now. "Stephen gave me some credit," she murmured wonderingly. "Did you hear him, Gran?"

"What a funny one you are," Gran said. "Don't you know that he has always thought you were plenty smart? But he'd feel foolish showing it. Boys are like that. He was pretty upset when we couldn't find you."

The waiting seemed very long, yet it couldn't have been more than twenty minutes, when Sumiko, who had gone back and forth from room to veranda several times, turned to them in excitement.

"Here they come!" she cried. "And I think they've found something!"

The boys came racing up the stairs and each one carried in his hands a long, earth-encrusted object.

"Just a second," Gran cried, "before you go sprinkling dirt all over our clean *tatami*." She went into her room and was back in a minute with an old copy of the newspaper *Mainichi*. As she spread the newspaper out on the floor, Stephen told how they had tried digging in one or two places, and then Hiro had suggested the space under the stairs as being a likely spot for hiding something. So there they had dug and these two long narrow parcels were what they had found, buried not too far beneath the surface.

The outer wrapping was of Japanese oiled paper and it had held up very well in the earth of the bomb shelter.

Hiro got his piece unwound first and sat staring at the strange-looking object in his hand. It bore the shape of the upper part of a sword, guard and all, but it was completely encrusted with some dried blackish stuff, the surface of which could be picked off in bits with the fingers. Stephen's piece looked like the lower end of the sword, but it too was covered with the thick black stuff.

Stephen lifted it to his nose. " I think it's tar," he said. " Your father must have covered the sword with this stuff before he buried it."

Hiro nodded. " This to protect blade so no rust destroys. Tar can be removed."

" Sure it can," Stephen said. " It will take a lot of work, but I'll help you. Maybe we can heat the stuff to soften it. Maybe kerosene will help. Gran, do you suppose — "

Gran shook her head, smiling. " Not tonight, dear. It's a big project, and once you get started, you won't want to stop. When it's clean and the *menuki* have been put in place again, Hiro, you can return the sword to your grandfather."

Hiro's face did not brighten. All the excitement had gone out of him. He gestured sadly toward the two pieces. " Blade is broken," he said. " When all honor goes from Japan, my father breaks the blade. How I am to show this sad thing to Grandfather? "

" It's best to show him," Gran said. " You mustn't try to pretend any more. After all, your grandfather ordered the sword destroyed completely. He should be glad to have any of it back."

Hiro was not so sure, but they left it at that. He and Sumiko said good night and went home across the alley.

" Hey, kid, how you feeling? " Stephen asked Celia, leaning over to tug at a fair strand of her hair.

" I'm fine," she murmured, and she really was.

"What a wonderful story!" Gran said. "There could be a whole chapter in my book about the Samurai Ghost and the finding of the sword . . . and I can't use a word of it."

"Why can't you?" Stephen's tone was blank.

Gran and Celia looked at each other understandingly. Celia knew the answer, even if Stephen didn't. Almost everything could be told to Gentaro Sato — all about the finding of the clues, the digging in the bomb shelter, the discovery of the sword. But they could never, never tell him that his own grandson had impersonated the family samurai. That one thing must be left to the old man's belief. Perhaps it was the only thing that would compensate for the breaking of the sword. Now the spirit would never appear again and Mr. Sato would be sure it was at rest. It would be too upsetting for him to know the truth. Thus it could never be printed in a book.

"Never mind," Gran said. "I'd rather live a mystery than write one anyway."

"But why do you think Hiro's father did these strange things?" Celia pondered.

"That's beyond the understanding of someone who isn't Japanese," she said. "But I've talked to many people who lived through the end of war and who were terribly afraid of the coming Occupation. They didn't know what we would be like. Thousands of people buried the few valuables they had clung to through the war in secret hiding places when our soldiers came in."

"But we wouldn't have taken them," Stephen said scornfully.

"How could they know that?" Gran asked. "In a few weeks of course they were digging things up again, realizing that our soldiers weren't going to harm anyone. Perhaps because Gentaro Sato had ordered him to destroy the sword, Hiro's father didn't want to tell anyone that he hadn't obeyed. But he had to hide it so that it wouldn't fall into what he regarded as enemy hands."

She paused in her thinking out loud, and softly Celia took up the story.

"Maybe Hiro's father had a feeling even then that he might not return, Gran. So he left these things behind to point the way. But he wouldn't want to point too easily to the sword, so he made the directions into two steps. That way he could leave the first clues under the false bottom of the lacquer box. Perhaps his family knew the box trick and he expected them to find the things and understand what they meant, though outsiders wouldn't. He couldn't know that his family would move out of this house and leave it for the Americans, and that the lacquer box would be left behind in a storeroom."

Gran nodded. "It could be that way. We'll never know for sure. Apparently it took an American girl with a taste for mystery to find the possible answers."

Stephen whistled in agreement. "I'll say it did! You really figured things out, Ceria-san. But next time wait for me, so you won't hurt yourself falling downstairs."

He was looking at her with affection, and Celia felt her own warm love for her brother surge up anew. She understood about Stephen now.

"Anyway the show's over," he said and yawned widely.

"No," said Celia. "It's not over. It can't be over until that sword is in Mr. Sato's hands and we know how he feels about it."

But more than a week passed and the night of the Daimonji bonfire had come before that was possible.

The X-rays had shown no serious damage and Celia was up again, her ankle taped and fairly comfortable. It would have been terrible not to be up for this occasion because Gentaro Sato had sent them a very special invitation. From the veranda of his present house an excellent view of the biggest bonfire would be possible, and he had asked Celia and Stephen and their grandmother to do him the honor of visiting him that evening.

Something else was to be accomplished as well. Stephen and Hiro had worked hard at cleaning and polishing the sword. Gran had found a craftsman who had replaced the tiny gold-and-silver dragons in their place on each side of the hilt. The pieces of long steel blade shone when they caught the light, and only Celia shivered when she looked at them.

She could not forget the history of this sword. It had been used in fighting. Perhaps it had even taken human life. In her eyes it was a terrifying thing and she did not like to touch it. Stephen said the blade was very sharp and she'd better stay away from it or she'd be sure to cut herself.

In the end, however, it was decided — through a conference attended by Hiro and Sumiko — that it was Celia who must bring the sword on the night of Daimonji and present it to Gentaro Sato. The prospect frightened her a little because she was fearful of what might happen when she gave the broken sword to Mr. Sato.

Gran thought he ought to be told the story of the sword's rediscovery first, but Hiro shook his head over that. His grandfather was still weak and worried and the one solid thing in his world would be the sword. Let him see it first and let it come to him, in a sense, from America. This would be a good thing.

So that evening, when they dressed in their best and went across the alley to the Sato house, Celia carried the pieces of the sword, carefully wrapped in a green silk *furoshiki*.

Sumiko met them at the door and Celia stared in astonishment. Tonight her friend wore a lovely kimono, with peach blossoms scattered across the cloth, and a gold-colored obi tied in the traditional manner above her waist. Only the pony tail was American, and it bobbed saucily as Sumiko went down on her knees to greet them with a deep bow and welcome them in Japanese. Her eyes were dancing when she raised her head, and she jumped up in a very un-Japanese manner.

"How do you like me?" she cried, and turned all the way around for their approval. In the background her mother hovered, and Hiro's mother, and Mr. Sato's daughter, all smiling in delight over Sumiko's transformation.

"You look perfect, Sumiko," Gran said. "A kimono becomes you."

"I don't know if it does or not." Sumiko looked straight into Gran's eyes. "I wouldn't wear one all the time. But I've been thinking about the things you said and I had a long talk with my grandfather the other day. He listened as I never expected he would. Maybe because I never gave him a chance before. I told him what you said about my needing to be both a good American and a good Japanese, Mrs. Bronson, and I think he is trying very hard to understand that idea. So I'm wearing this kimono to please him tonight."

There was affection in the look Gran gave her. "Pleasing someone else is probably the first step we all have to take in order to please ourselves. To like ourselves," she said.

Sumiko flashed a bright smile and padded ahead of them upstairs in her split-toed white *tabi*, her walk as demure as that of any old-fashioned Japanese girl.

Up the steep stairs after her went Celia, uneasily carrying the *furoshiki* bundle in both hands. Gentaro Sato sat before his painting things, but when Sumiko went down on her knees to bow to him, he stood up to greet his guests. Celia thought he looked pleased and a little proud as his eyes fell on Sumiko. Then he was bowing to Gran as Sumiko introduced her.

Zabuton — cushions — had been set around the big room of mats and everyone sat down. Only Hiro, Celia saw, was even more nervous than she, and his eyes hardly left his grandfather's face. Tonight meant a great deal to Hiro.

When the inevitable tea had been brought and the small cups passed around, as well as the little flowerlike cakes that Celia liked, Mr. Sato made a brief speech of welcome, which Sumiko translated. Then Hiro could wait no longer.

" I tell him now," he said. " I tell him Ceria-san is bringing him gift." And he spoke in Japanese to his grandfather.

The old man turned his benevolent look upon Celia, smiled, and waited.

Now that the moment had come, Celia found her hands trembling as she turned back the silken folds of the *furoshiki*. Were they doing the right thing after all? Would the sight of this sword be too great a shock for the old man, coming suddenly like this? But she could hesitate no longer. The moment was here. She let the last fold of cloth fall away from the gleaming broken blade,-the handsome, gold-inlaid hilt of the sword.

Gentaro stared for a moment, his face expressionless. Then he bent forward from the waist and, taking the hilt in his hand, picked up the broken upper section of the sword. Very carefully he turned it about, examining the *menuki* in recognition. He knew, plainly, that this was the samurai sword that had come down through his fam-

ily. The very sword whose destruction he had ordered so
many years ago when Japan had reached her most terrible
moment in history. In grave inquiry his eyes rested upon
Celia and she spoke anxiously to Hiro.

" Tell him, Hiro. Tell him quickly! "

Gran lifted her teacup, pretending not to watch, while
Hiro spoke, and Celia knew that was best. They all sat
sipping hot, bitter green tea while Hiro told his grandfather the story, in lengthy Japanese. Once the old man
exclaimed and glanced at Celia, and to her relief she saw
the corner of his mouth lift in a faint smile. Hiro, with gestures, had come to the place where Celia had fallen down
the stairs. But Celia knew that not all of the rescue would
be related. The fact that Hiro had come through the tunnel into the shelter would play no part in this story, for
no suspicion of the trick that Hiro had played must ever
cross his grandfather's mind.

When it was all told, the old man sat quietly for a moment, and Celia saw that his eyes were moist with tears.
Undoubtedly he was thinking of his son, who could not
bear to destroy this sword, even at the order of the father
he revered. Then he spoke a few words to Sumiko and
she went quickly to the cupboard and brought out the
stand with the sword sheath upon it.

Gentaro Sato picked up the sheath and dropped the
broken blade into the bottom of it. Then he placed the
upper part of the sword in the sheath as well. Now it sat
upon the stand looking whole, with the handsome hilt
protruding at one end.

Hiro translated the grave words of thanks Gentaro Sato
spoke to Celia.

" My grandfather says it is good that sword is broken.
Japan lives in friendship now. There is more honor in clasp
of hand than in stroke of sword."

Gran went impulsively to kneel beside him and held out her hand in American fashion. Gentaro Sato took it in his and bowed over it, combining the Eastern and Western salute. He spoke to her and this time it was Sumiko who translated excitedly.

"He thanks you for coming, Mrs. Bronson. And he wishes to know if your gifted and clever granddaughter might be permitted to come to him for painting lessons in the Japanese manner while she is here in Kyoto."

Celia gasped and Gran said: "How wonderful! Tell him how grateful we are, Sumiko. There's nothing I know that would please Celia more."

Before Sumiko had finished, there was a scampering on the stairs, and up came little Joto, the two Mrs. Satos, and the daughter as well, with Kimi and Kiku following. They all bowed respectfully to Mr. Sato and then chattered to him like so many birds.

Sumiko jumped up. "It's almost time for the bonfires to be lighted. We must all go out on the veranda so we won't miss what's going to happen."

Everyone stood back to let Gentaro Sato go first, then his guests followed, and finally the members of the household. The gallery was narrow, but when the *zabuton* were brought they could all sit in a line, stretching the length of it. Celia found herself next to Gentaro Sato, with Sumiko on her other side. Gran sat on Mr. Sato's right, with Hiro beyond her.

Below spread the lights of Kyoto, cupped in the dark, reaching arms of the hills. Then, with a suddenness that was startling, a switch was thrown and every light in the city went out. The night was black velvet — sky and earth and city, all one vast expanse of darkness.

High on the slope of Mt. Daimonji, wood had been

gathered for days. It was piled in a pit dug in the shape of the Japanese character "*dai*," which means "great." Now, near this pit, appeared the flare of a torch, followed by another false flare or two. Suddenly there was a tremendous burst of flame on the mountainside, as the entire bonfire exploded into the great flaming character.

Celia drew in her breath sharply. The sight was so strange and beautiful. Mountain and city and sky were invisible. There was only that vast burning character floating there in space.

Stephen pointed to where other bonfires had now been lighted, but none was so great or impressive as this one.

Celia glanced at Gentaro Sato beside her, and saw that his attention was fixed, not upon the bonfire, but upon the garden across the way. Though there was no need now to try to pierce the darkness, to look for the strange figure of a ghostly samurai. How would he feel, she wondered, now that the figure would never appear again? Would he be satisfied because the sword had been returned to its proper place of honor?

What she saw in the face of Gentaro Sato startled her. He was staring at the garden as if in recognition. As if something moved there that her own eyes could not see. As she watched, he bowed his head courteously in the direction of the garden, and it was as if he were saying *sayonara*. She strained to see if there was anything there in the shadows, but nothing was visible to her intent gaze. Yet the old man looked pleased and happy — content.

Sumiko had not seen. She whispered to Celia: "So now Daimonji is over. But there are still more festivals to come. And there's a month of summer left. Oh, I'm glad we're here together, Celia!"

Celia slipped her hand into her friend's and squeezed it.

She didn't need to put her own feelings into words. A whole month was left, and there were still so many things she and Sumiko could do. And there were her painting lessons with the grandfather to enjoy.

Kyoto, Japan, she thought dreamily. *It's now and I'm here. And I'll remember it forever.*

About Phyllis A. Whitney

$\mathcal{U}$NTIL I was fifteen years old my home was in the Orient. I was born in Yokohama, Japan, and lived in Japan, China, and the Philippines during those years. Since I remember the Orient very well, I have always wanted to return for a visit. There was no opportunity, however, until recently when my husband and I made a vacation trip to the places where I had lived as a child.

Japan was the country I remembered best and most wanted to write about, so we planned to spend the greater part of our vacation there. I felt that Kyoto would make an especially fascinating background for a book because it was never destroyed by bombs as some of the other cities were. In ancient times Kyoto was the capital of Japan, and many of the shrines and temples date back hundreds of years.

My purpose was to write about American children in the Orient, since that is the life I know best. I found several American families living in Kyoto on Fulbright Fellowships, and the young people in these families were interested in my book and eager to tell me about their experiences in Japan. The three boys to whom this book is dedicated were among my most enthusiastic helpers.

Of course I wanted to give an authentic picture of Japanese life as well, and was fortunate in having Japanese friends who invited us to their homes and explained many facets of Japanese life.

In Kyoto I was introduced to a well-known artist and visited his home, where he painted a lovely picture for me, just as the artist in the story does for Celia. The visit to the movie studio was another real adventure, although it was not so exciting in real life as it could be made in a story.

Perhaps that is the most satisfying thing about writing fiction. I am able to live again the wonderful experiences I have had in distant places, and yet I can make them doubly exciting through the adventures of my characters.